a specie

A Memory of Murder

A Jan Christopher Mystery

Helen Hollick

Helen Hollick [signature]

quiz night
at the Exeter
Inn!

5.5.24

TAW RIVER
PRESS

A MEMORY OF MURDER
A Jan Christopher Mystery - Episode 5
By Helen Hollick

ISBN
978-1-7392720-2-9 (Paperback)
978-1-7392720-3-6 (e-book)

Published by Taw River Press
https://www.tawriverpress.co.uk

"A delicious distraction... What a lovely way to spend an afternoon!"

"I really identified with Jan – the love of stories from an early age, and the careers advice – the same reaction I got – no one thought being a writer was something a working class girl did! The character descriptions are wonderfully done."

"Brilliant! I'm so enjoying Helen's well-researched murder mystery. I'm not giving anything away here, except to say there's lots of nostalgia, and detail that readers of a certain age (me included) will lap up. A jolly good read. In my opinion, it would make a great television series."

PRAISE FOR A MEADOW MURDER
(episode 4)

(Devon, England 1972)

"As delicious as a Devon Cream Tea!" *author Elizabeth St John*

"An easy gentle read with likeable, well developed characters, and an atmospheric plot set around the farming and equestrian communities. I really enjoyed the nostalgic element and also the vivid, affectionate evocation of the rural Devon landscape. Highly recommended for anyone who enjoyed cozy crime stories set in rural England." *author Debbie Young*

"Every sentence pulls you back into the early 1970s... The Darling Buds of May, but Devon not Kent. The countryside itself is a character and Hollick imbues it with plenty of emotion." *author Alison Morton*

To Annie
A very successful author, and one of my dearest friends

1

HOW IT BEGAN

Thursdays at the public library in Hall Lane, Chingford, were never looked forward to with much relish by the staff. Even now, from where I'm writing my memoirs, (if you can call recording my ordinary life during those distant days of the 1970s as 'memoirs'), I clearly remember how difficult it was to get out of bed on a Thursday morning and head off to work. I was twenty years old in April 1973, no longer a teenager but still too trusting and far too naïve about life in general despite being the ward of my uncle, Detective Chief Inspector Toby Christopher, and engaged to his Detective Sergeant, Lawrence – Laurie – Walker. I think many of us were 'unworldly' back then, with no modern social media platforms or multiple TV channels to open our eyes to what happened beyond; in my case, a small patch of suburban North London life.

We had one telephone in the hall at home, no mobile phones, no computers or internet. Goodness, I recall being as proud as punch of my new stereo system that I had received for my birthday in January, a

Dolby system with Wharfedale speakers. Don't laugh, I still have those speakers; I'm listening to a Golden Oldie through them as I write this. *Dark Side of the Moon* by Pink Floyd, first released in the spring of 1973. Most houses only had the one TV. I was lucky as I had a black and white set in my small sitting room which adjoined my bedroom and my own small bathroom. Uncle Toby and Aunt Madge's house was quite large in a reasonably affluent area of North Chingford, and I'd lived with them ever since they'd adopted me when I was orphaned at five years old. After I became engaged to Laurie, Aunt Madge converted one of the spare rooms into a sitting room to make a sort of partial self-contained flat where Laurie and I could be more private. She didn't approve of Laurie moving in with me, though. The occasional discreet overnight stay was one thing, but until we were married, appearances had to be kept up, not because of any prudishness, but because of any possible unpleasant scandal. Policemen were supposed to have high moral standards. Laurie and my uncle certainly did, but sad to say, there were too many among the police who had their own less than ethical principles, and too many busybodies who could make two Mount Everests out of one tiny molehill.

For myself: I was born prematurely at the end of January 1953, and named January for the month, but I prefer everyone to call me Jan. My twin sister, who died when I was three, got June for when we were conceived. I still envy her the better name.

Thursdays were school days at the library. Junior school visits from the school opposite. Some of the kids were OK, several were little monsters. Add to that, on this particular Thursday they were all over excited.

I will never forget that Thursday in April, nor the couple of weeks which followed. You don't expect a missing child and a murder to mess up Easter with its fancy chocolate eggs and furry Easter bunnies, do you? Nor do you expect long-buried memories to resurface with all the force of a cork popping out of a fizzed-up bottle of Champagne...

2

A LITTLE MISTAKE

I made a dreadful error on Thursday morning. Stupid of me, but one of those things where you speak first, engage mushy brain after, and wish you'd kept quiet a few awkward seconds later. My turn to be in charge of date stamping the books the class visit children chose to take home with them. I sat at the round table in the children's library trying to hear myself think – the days of 'silence in the library' were long gone, which was good in most instances, but thirty or so almost-eleven-year-olds in the relatively small area of the children's section can make a surprisingly huge amount of noise.

Most of the boys messed about, not interested in books. A few were keen on the football and aeroplane books, one lad took a Biggles story, another the latest Doctor Who adventure, but the rest, I could tell, were random choices made to please the teacher more than anything else. The girls were more enthusiastic; they usually made a bee line for the books about pets and animals, or Enid Blyton. I never could understand the attraction of Blyton's boarding school stories, but then school had not been the best of experiences for me. I checked out a third book about Malory Towers – we stocked two copies of the six-book series – and guessed that some sort of minor fad was trending between the girls. I called these sort of young ladies 'The Frilly Knicker Brigade' when I was at secondary school. Posh girls with neat, clean, sensible shoes and a spotless uniform with the pleated navy-blue skirt at a regulation quarter inch above the knee. And a superior attitude towards anyone they saw as beneath them socially. That had definitely included me because I didn't have a proper mum or dad and I was shy and quiet. Add in that my uncle was a copper and you have a ready-made magnet for the bullies. The best day of my life was the day I left school and was rid of their tormenting.

Not that any of this applied to these particular junior school kids, not yet anyway, although they would probably change once they went up to grammar or secondary school. In my experience, too many junior school children had the inherent propensity to turn into misogynists, or arrogant madams once senior school and the teenage years kicked in. Admitted, this particular class wasn't a bad lot, just over excited.

Their teacher apologised again. "They are already excited about breaking up for the Easter holiday tomorrow, and are well over-the-top from the visitors we had at school yesterday. Some of the performers from the circus on Chingford Plain came to show us their skills. We had acrobats and clowns in a makeshift arena set out with straw bales in the playground. A few horses trotted round, then we had some dogs and chimps. The children loved it, but we, the teachers have to keep some sort of ordered discipline now. I can't say I approve of circuses, and this was undoubtedly a ruse to attract more audience to the real Big Top. How many of the little darlings are now begging their parents to see the whole show? No, Nigel, William doesn't want that book stuffed down his trousers. Stop it."

I date stamped the next Blyton book, noticing it was the only one I had actually read when I was younger and not so discerning about quality reading. It had a girl called Wilhelmina Robinson who adored horses, with her own horse, Thunder, stabled at the school during term time. I'd read it because of the horse, even if Thunder was not a very imaginative name, and why did she have a *horse* not a *pony*? (Horse people will know there is a huge difference. Horses are for grown-ups, ponies are for kids.) And what about travel practicalities? Transporting horses is not as easy as catching the next bus! OK, truth time. Blyton annoyed me.

"Do you like horses?" I asked the girl who was borrowing the book, who by coincidence, was Wendy Robinson. Better than Wilhelmena I suppose.

She shook her head. "Not particularly."

"But you like school stories?" I broadened my friendly, engaging, library assistant smile.

Again she shook her head. "Not really."

I faltered slightly. "Why choose this book then?"

"Because Mummy doesn't like me reading Enid Blyton, she says she is a trite writer. So I chose this one to annoy her."

A fair enough reason I suppose, although I agreed with Mummy.

Then I made my faux pas with the next girl in the queue. She was a very little girl, much smaller than any of the others. Stupidly, I said to her, "Goodness, when are you going to grow bigger?"

I didn't get an answer. She simply stared at me a moment as if I was the wicked witch from *The Wizard of Oz* and walked off with her book, *Huckleberry Finn* which was, I thought, a rather unusual choice as, although it was a classic, Mark Twain wasn't a popular author for British children.

It was at that point I realised she was a dwarf. I kicked myself for my insensitivity but couldn't go after her to apologise as the teacher wanted to get finished and be gone. Would you believe the teacher's name was Miss Grayling, another Malory Towers connection.

To add to the chaos as the children were noisily lining up, two of the decorators arrived. The library was to have a thorough paint overhaul, with the revolting avocado green walls being turned into a more pleasing pale primrose yellow. The men were scheduled to start first thing Monday but had, it seemed, finished their previous job earlier than expected, so wondered if they could make a start on the morrow, Friday.

I happened to be the first person the gaffer and his mate saw as they wandered in from the back, staff, entrance. Bert, our caretaker, was not, I assumed, lurking in his cubbyhole otherwise the strangers would have been instantly intercepted.

"Can I help you?" I asked, looking at the decorators with one of my hard, disapproving stares while simultaneously ushering the last of the children into their crocodile line.

The smarter of the two men, in appearance, anyway, said, "Here about the paint job, Mrs?"

I didn't correct him about the 'Mrs'. "Oh. You aren't due until Monday."

The second man grinned at me. "Need to get goin' as soon as poss, love. Time's money, and what with Easter comin' up, to start a day early means we'll finish a day early, see?"

"Or at least, complete on time," the other man said.

"Joe here is off on holiday on the Saturday after we finish."

"Going to Bournemouth with my nephew for a week. Got a nice hotel on the Front booked. Henry here always gives us a bonus if we finish on time, don't you Henry? So we want to get everything spick and spam before we go." Joe explained.

That made sense. Apart from the spam. I think he meant span.

The second man, Joe, whistled tunelessly through his teeth as he gazed at the library layout. "Phew, there's a fair few curtain hooks here in't there? People read 'em all, miss?"

Curtain hooks? Was this Cockney rhyming slang for books?

"Most of them – Charlie, leave those tickets alone and get into line. Miss Grayling is ready to go." I reached forward and snatched the bundle of pink junior tickets from young Charlie's grubby mitt, hoped the little so-an'-so hadn't swapped any of the book charge cards around. If he had we'd have a right task sorting out which child had borrowed which book at their next visit. Charlie promptly grabbed the date stamp and pressed it to the back of his hand, leaving an inky smudge on what was not particularly clean skin. His shirt was hanging out from the back of his short trousers and his hair was clearly a stranger to a comb. I moved back from him when I'm sure I saw something scuttle amongst its untidy tangle. (I was scratching at my scalp for the rest of the day, and washed my hair three times the moment I got home. And I bet, having read that sentence you're now scalp-scratching as well. Lice are like yawns – catching!)

"You want the librarian, Miss Pamela Bower," I said to the two decorators as I pointed up the library to where she sat at her desk. Miss Grayling and her charges were, thankfully, all filing out through the main doors. Charlie and his lice included. Another Thursday visit done and dusted.

"Looks like she's busy on the phone," the first man, Henry – the owner of the decorating firm, I later found out – responded as he finished glancing around the building. The library was basically one large rectangular room, divided in half at the centre by the u-shaped wooden counter for receiving in and stamping out library books. To one side of it the main entrance doors and surrounding glass-windowed lobby, to the other, two desks, the shorter one being the librarian's desk, the longer counter for the business of the music library.

To one side of the adult library, an alcoved area formed the small reference library with its adjoining reading area which was carpeted and set with comfortable chairs and low coffee-tables. We stocked quite a good selection of popular magazines and a range of daily newspapers from *The Times* to the *Daily Mirror*, but excluding *The Sun* because of its unsuitable page-three content of semi-naked busty women.

The man called Joe sniffed and wiped at his nose. "High ceilings. I don't much like high ceilings, gives me verdigris."

"I think you mean vertigo?" I corrected as I walked towards the main counter, tray of junior tickets and the date stamp in hand. "Miss Bower looks like she's free now," I added, grateful that Pam had looked up and already spotted us.

I left them to it, concentrated on counting the tickets to show how many books had been discharged to the class, then took myself back into the children's half to tidy the shelves into some sort of semblance of library order.

Some dear child had re-arranged a section of books

back to front with the pages facing out, not the spines. I had to laugh; the books were all on the temporary display shelf devoted to – in this case – children's mystery stories. Whoever that child was, he or she undoubtedly had a witty sense of humour and an innovative imagination! Mystery stories indeed, as no one could see any of the titles.

3

NO TIME FOR TEA

I was somewhat surprised when at 6.40 my fiancé, DS
Laurie Walker tapped on the staffroom door. Surprised
and embarrassed, for he caught me out. Win –
Winifred, but we all called her Win – was in the process
of pouring mugs of tea for herself, me and our music
librarian, Simon – who preferred to be called Sy. Win
was part time, and Simon was in charge of the sound
recordings which mostly consisted of vinyl LPs, but we
were expanding with the acquisition of cassette tapes.
Sy was twenty-two, trending towards dressing like a
tidy hippy (I know, a *tidy* hippy is hard to believe!) and
was in a band.

"Hello Laurie," Win chirruped, brandishing the
teapot. "Want a cuppa?"

We'd had our long tea break, a chance to eat before
the evening shift, between 4.30 and 5 p.m, but I was
always peckish these two hours later so, even though I
was supposed to be keeping an eye on what I ate, I
devoured my sandwiches at the first break and enjoyed
a cake or chocolate bar during this later one. To my
consternation, Laurie had now discovered my guilty
secret! Although I suspected that as my waistline was

not decreasing, he probably guessed it anyway. I hastily stuffed the remains of the large Bakewell Tart into my mouth, and crossed my fingers in hope that he wouldn't say anything. Too much to hope that he hadn't noticed – he was a policeman, and a policeman trained by my Detective Chief Inspector uncle to be a very observant one.

We took it in turns to take the post up to the post office of an afternoon and stopped off at the café in Albert Crescent to get the evening staff sandwiches or, as in my case, a cake. Sy had gone this afternoon because he'd had some of his own shopping to get which, strictly speaking, we shouldn't do in work time, but we all did.

I chewed and swallowed quickly as I got up from my chair to offer Laurie a somewhat crumbly kiss. "We've only just started our tea break," I said, "good timing!"

Laurie kissed me back but declined the tea. "Can't stop, and I'm afraid I'm here on official business."

That sounded ominous. I know I wasn't supposed to be eating fattening cakes, but that was hardly against the law!

"If you're enquiring about the rave that took place on Wanstead Flats last Saturday night," Sy said, looking up from his copy of *New Musical Express*, "I wasn't there."

"I'd say that only people who *were* there would know about it," Laurie answered. "It was a wash out apparently. By all accounts, the music could hardly be heard, and what could be heard was dreadful."

"That's what comes of amateurs running these things, and not having quality equipment," Sy retorted. I did wonder if he was telling the truth about not being there. How else would he know about the equipment?

I'm sure I was imagining it, but had I picked up,

several months ago soon after Simon had joined the library staff, that Laurie didn't like him? I think the feeling was mutual, for whenever they did meet they were like grumpy cats sparring over which one was entitled to use the cat flap first. In my opinion, Sy was nice. Most of his hippy, 'Love and Peace man!' trendiness was put on to go along with his rock band image. I had discovered, purely by chance, that his passion, apart from his beloved best guitar – an expensive Fender Stratocaster – was for opera, Shakespeare and Bach.

I recall Sy making me laugh the week he'd joined the staff when he'd said that Shakespeare had probably enjoyed his schooldays because he'd not had to study Shakespeare.

Even though Laurie had said no to the tea, Win still poured a mugful and handed it to him. He took a gulp but didn't sit down. "You had a school class in today, I believe?" he asked.

"Yes, Miss Grayling's 4G from Chase Lane Junior," I answered as I sat down again, trying not to look longingly at the book I'd been reading and hiding my very brief expression of annoyance, while hoping that, again, Laurie hadn't noticed. I loved him dearly, of course, but anyone who knows what I mean about being engrossed in a really good book will have every sympathy for such opposing tugs of loyalty.

This tea break was only twenty minutes, so I didn't have long to read, and I was almost at the end of the book. I desperately wanted to know how it ended. One of the perks of being a library assistant, we had first dibs when new books came in. Although this one had actually been published in 1970 it had remained pretty obscure until word of mouth rocketed it into the best seller charts. I loved it and wanted my own copy; I'd been dropping heavy hints for it as an Easter present from my Aunt Madge and Uncle Toby. *Jonathan Livingston Seagull* by Richard Bach is quirky I suppose, seeing as it is about a seagull, Jonathan, an independent thinker frustrated with the squabbles over hunting for food with his flock of noisy gulls who have no sense of purpose. Jonathan has a passion for experimenting with flight, and wants to learn more about his own body, the environment and the meaning of life. Believe me, it's not as silly as it sounds. Read it.

"We've had a report that one of the children didn't arrive home after school," Laurie said, finishing his tea in two great swallows. "It's early, not yet seven, but she should have been home three hours ago. We've established that she left school at the normal time and started walking her usual way home, which would have brought her past the library." He had a policeman's questioning tone to his voice, 'interview technique' my uncle called it. "She's Sally Armitage. Miss Bower, your librarian, said just now that you went shopping this afternoon, Mr Henbury-Clive? I'm just checking whether you noticed anything unusual at all while you were out?"

Sy shook his head. "Call me Sy. Mr Henbury-Clive sounds so upper class snobby. I can't say as I remember anything out of the ordinary. Kids doing things that kids always do. Younger ones wanting sweets from their mums, older kids hanging around outside Maynard's tobacconist and sweetshop next to the cinema, hoping to cadge fags off their elders."

Did I see a slight red tinge to his cheeks? Sy smoked, although not heavily, but enough to have a slight whiff of tobacco clinging to his clothes. He never smoked here at work. Well, if he did it was in the gents' loo or out the back on the small patch of overgrown wasteland.

I'd paled at the mention of the name. Sally

Armitage. That was the little girl, the one I'd so unintentionally upset about her lack of height. Because of my embarrassment I was not going to admit my unintentional rudeness in front of my work colleagues, or Laurie, but it immediately swept through my mind: had she run away, was she hiding somewhere dreadfully upset because of my inappropriateness?

"Was everything all right when she left school?" I queried.

"Apparently. According to her class teacher Sally seemed her normal self. Bubbling about the forthcoming Easter holidays and looking forward to enjoying herself."

"Sally was OK when she was here," I said truthfully, but not mentioning the girl's discomfort at my clumsiness. "A bit quiet, but shy little girls usually are." I bit my lip. I'd done it again! *Little*.

"Her smallness puts her at a disadvantage," Win explained, speaking for us all. "The other children tease her because of her smallness."

And library assistants saying stupid things don't help, I thought.

Laurie took out his pencil and black notebook from his jacket pocket to read through some previously taken notes. "Her teacher didn't mention that she was shy, in fact the opposite, rather chatty and always full of impractical ideas. She wants to be an actress when she leaves school."

"I just assumed she was shy, because she keeps herself to herself," I explained.

"Maybe she's simply wary of us grown ups?" Win suggested. She had probably hit the nail on the head.

Laurie glanced at his notebook. "A couple of the parents we've managed to contact said they saw her walking towards the library straight after leaving school, so that would have been just after 3.30.

Presumably she was on her way home, but we wondered if perhaps she'd come in here at all?"

"I left to take the post at about 3.15," Sy said. "Straight to the post office, queued for a good ten minutes. Went across to Boots over the road, then the café and Maynard's. Got back here about 4.20."

An hour, where he should have taken half that time, but we all dawdled when it was our turn to escape for a while.

"Those of us who work in the evening are in the office of an afternoon, unless we're short staffed," I said, "so we wouldn't have noticed anything in the library or outside. I could look through the tickets to see if she came in for another book, but as she'd been in earlier with the school it's highly unlikely."

"I think your colleagues out on the counter are already doing that," Laurie said.

"Was she walking by herself then?" Sy queried, his brows inverted into a disapproving frown. "A bit young to be on her tod, isn't she?"

"She's nearly eleven, and according to her library membership card, lives in Marmion Avenue, a couple of houses down from here, so not far to go," I protested. "The Lollipop Lady sees the children across the main road, so most who live nearby walk to and from school on their own. I did from when I was about eight, mind, we didn't live along the Ridgeway then, we were in Heriot, up the top of the Mount. We moved when Uncle Toby became a DCI. The Lollipop Lady would be a good person to ask." I suggested the last to Laurie.

"We're tracking her down," he responded in a tone that was not too hopeful of a useful answer.

"Am I suspect for kidnap?" Sy asked with a tinge of hostility. "If I am, I must have moved P.D.Q., to do the post *and* the shopping, *and* kidnap a girl *and* spirit her away. You can search my locker if you like," he jerked his thumb over his shoulder at the grey metal lockers of ours. "Ask at the café and Maynard's. They both know me well, they'll confirm I was there."

Laurie nodded but didn't smile as he put his notebook away. "I'll forgo the locker, but for the rest, I will do, sir. To enquire is routine procedure, part of my job in this sort of case."

Sy shrugged. "Parents shouldn't let their kids out on their own," added with a disgruntled sniff. "Asking for trouble, that is."

"Not all parents are able to escort their children to and fro," Laurie replied equally as disgruntled. Why did these two rub each other the wrong way? Testosterone had a lot to answer for. "Not all parents have cars, and several mums have to work these days."

I thought his answer was sharp, but in this instance I agreed with him, so I added, "She'll be going up to big school in September, so walking to school on her own then."

"Didn't you walk to school at that age?" Win asked Sy.

He laughed ruefully. "I went to boarding school from when I was seven, so I only had the grand oak staircase to walk down to get to class each day. Or the dorm window to shin out of when we were able to secretly bunk off."

"Anyway, that's all beside the point," Laurie said masking a gruff snort, "I'll be getting off. We've more people to ask, more places to search."

Was his gruffness because he was uncomfortable about the boarding school reference, or the awful fact of a child being packed off by his unloving parents? Not that I knew whether Sy's parents were unloving or not.

"Have you taken a look out the back?" I suggested

to Laurie. "It's only a small waste ground area, but you never know. And it more-or-less backs onto her house. Maybe she plays there, she wouldn't be the first child to have a secret den amongst all that tangled overgrowth."

"It's getting dark out there, but I had a quick shufty before I came in here," Laurie said, patting his pocket where I could see the shape of a torch. "You seem to have a rather large pile of ladders, scaffolding boards and tins of paint covered up by a tarpaulin out there. Any child would need the hide of a rhinoceros because there's enough nettles to supply a witch's cauldron for several months' worth of potions, but we'll make a proper search tomorrow in daylight." He looked pale and drawn, dark rings already forming under his eyes. Tiredness combined with worry. It had already been a long, difficult week for the local police with a series of violent burglaries, a spate of petty shoplifting and two rather horrific fatal road traffic accidents.

"Decorators," I explained about the paint pots and ladders. "They start work tomorrow instead of the expected Monday. They wanted to store everything somewhere indoors, but Pam objected. It's going to be bad enough having to shut off sections of the library and covering bookshelves, without them stacking all their paraphernalia in our way."

We were dreading the disruption and the inevitable complaining from the public. And now the worry of a young girl missing from home. I felt for her parents, but also for Laurie and my Uncle Toby.

The police would be making this case an essential priority, which meant that until, one way or another, she was found, there would be no chance of rest for any of them.

4

AN ACCUMULATION OF TOOT

Simon, Sy, usually gave me a lift home on Thursday nights, which was very good of him as where I lived was about ten minutes out of his way. Thursdays were his club night, although he never said what club or where it was. I assumed a music gig of some sort. He had a bright red, two-seater Lotus Elan which was sensational to look at, but very impractical being low to the ground and not that easy to get elegantly into, and even less elegantly out of. Having discovered that tight short skirts and Lotus seating did not go well together, I always made sure I wore trousers on Thursdays. Sy was a nice chap, with soft grey eyes and a wickedly funny sense of humour, but he was a bloke, and blokes like ogling a lady's thighs. At twenty-two he was younger than Laurie, although in my, admittedly biased opinion, not as handsome. He'd not been a member of staff all that long but had transformed the sound recording section almost overnight. It had previously consisted of mostly classical records, but he'd augmented the collection with quality rock, pop and folk, all of which was proving a hit with staff and the majority of the public, although we encountered a few grumbles from the fuddy-duddies who regarded anything that wasn't Mozart, Brahms or Wagner as a cacophony originating from the devil himself.

Sy was fashionably well dressed – trendy gear but not outrageous. He always wore a suit, shirt and tie to work, but with a hippy, snazzy waistcoat beneath his jacket. Today, the waistcoat and suit matched: bellbottomed trousers with a nicely cut jacket but the pattern was a loud houndstooth black and white check. His hair, I might add, was not long but not short, a sort of early Beatle-cut length to his collar. Sy was the lead guitarist in his band, but give him his due, he didn't pester for any of us to go along to any local gigs, although Laurie had taken me one recent Saturday evening when Sy was playing at the Royal Standard pub, opposite Blackhorse Road underground station. The group, The Sages of Thyme, were good, a mixture of rock and folk with a very slight hint of classical. Their version of *Scarborough Fair* had me in tears which was disastrous for my carefully applied mascara and eyeliner. I must have looked like I'd developed panda eyes. Laurie, not bothering to mask his amusement, had mopped me up with his handkerchief before the end of the gig, so I don't think anyone else noticed. The mascara ruined his white cotton hanky, I tried soaking it in Daz when we got home, but the black stains only turned grey and when I then bleached the darn thing, holes appeared so I bought him a set of four new ones from Woolworths.

Relieved to be going home after a long day at work, I slid into the passenger seat of the car, first removing two empty Dunhill cigarette packets and a pair of scruffy tennis shoes. Sy leaned over from the driver's side and took the items from me, dropping them onto an accumulating pile behind his seat.

"I don't know why I keep these old things," he

laughed, "I've only played tennis once since moving here from Aylesbury, and that was last week. Got roped into it by my younger brother who's staying with me at the moment. He's a pain, I can't wait for him to get off home to Mum. I'm running him back at the weekend, thank goodness."

"You've not much room in here for luggage?" I observed as he put the car in gear and roared off up Marmion Avenue and then turned right into Albert Crescent, mindful of a bus that was reversing into a parking space. Albert Crescent formed a temporary terminus for several bus routes, I think early on the entire layout had been purpose built for the trams that had once been the form of public transport, but don't quote me on that. With the facilities of the café on the corner, and the lavatories situated in the centre of the island Albert Crescent continued to serve as an ideal stopping point for bus drivers and conductors. Buses reversing into a parking space, or occasionally having to double park did tend to hold up other traffic. Not tonight, and the Hall Lane traffic lights were in our favour, so Sy put his foot down and we roared off. I noticed a few pedestrians scowling at us as we passed. Somewhat like a racing car, the Lotus did draw attention to itself by noisily announcing its presence.

With all the rubbish there wasn't much room for anything else. "Where do you put your guitar when heading for a gig?" I asked with genuine curiosity.

"Common misconception. An Elan's boot is quite spacious, room enough for a couple of medium-sized suitcases. As well as plenty of space behind the seats here for shoes, jackets – when it isn't taken up by all my discarded rubbish! I promise I'll clear it all out. Maybe one weekend."

"What? A weekend in the year 1999?"

He laughed. "You know what they say, 'Where there's a will'…"

I laughed and interrupted as I shifted my patchwork leather bag to sit more comfortably on my knee. It was far from full, but carried essentials – purse, keys, handkerchief, makeup and such. Oh, and *Jonathan Livingston Seagull*. I only had three pages left to read. "Do you mean the saying that goes; 'Where there's a will – I'd rather be on it?'"

Sy grinned. "Not heard that one before. Good one, I'll remember it. But even with my accumulated toot, I could probably squash a small body in the boot if I tried." Then he turned serious, realising what he'd inadvertently implied.

"Oh, crikey," he gulped, "that was bad taste wasn't it, given your fiancé's worrying news this evening? I do apologise. I have no idea about the poor girl, I truly didn't see her. Or if she was nearby, I didn't notice. I wasn't looking at the kids."

Bad taste indeed, but we were all capable of saying the wrong things at the wrong time. As I'd discovered.

"You were gone rather a long time, though," I ventured.

"Yes, well," Sy slowed to let an old couple cross the road at the zebra crossing near the Baptist Church, just over the brow of the Mount. "Truth to be told, I somewhat fancy that young lady in the Albert café. The one who wears those colourful headscarves. She has the most *gorgeous* almond-shaped eyes set against a pale olive skin. Her mother is Tunisian, so the exotic look is not unexpected. I, er," he reddened, embarrassed. "I spent a while chatting her up."

"Nothing wrong in that," I answered with a smile. "I agree she is quite beautiful."

"I'd prefer to keep the information to myself if you don't mind. It's not likely to get back to her, but Ma would have a seizure if she knew I was interested in someone of a mixed foreign race. She's rather a prig, my mater, and easily jumps to the wrong conclusions."

"Goodness! Talking to a pretty woman doesn't mean a wedding's going to take place tomorrow!" I exclaimed.

"Alas, it does in my family."

"Not in this case. Haven't you noticed the wedding ring on her finger? She's already married with three children."

Sy looked crestfallen. He sighed heavily. "Oh. No, I hadn't. That explains why she wasn't interested in coming out for a drink with me one evening."

"That and the fact that she's a Muslim, so doesn't touch alcohol."

The crestfallen expression fell even further, then he laughed. "I'm an idiot aren't I? I just thought the headscarf was a fashion thing."

"You don't know even the basics of different religions?" I was rather taken aback at his unexpected ignorance. He knew languages and music, literature – highbrow stuff but not the general everyday things. He reminded me of a cousin of Aunt Madge, a Cambridge Don, very highly educated but hadn't a clue about how to put oil in a car, open a bank account or even change a lightbulb. I couldn't help but feel slightly sorry for Sy. Maybe his posh family background wasn't as acceptable to him either? My dilemma: did I divulge all this to Laurie or keep quiet? I said, to change the subject slightly, "Perhaps they've found Sally by now?" I hoped that being positive would ease the slight chill of tension that had crept into the car.

My other thought was that maybe he wasn't as stupid as he was pretending to be and everything he'd said was a pack of lies.

Outside my house, (Uncle Toby and Aunt Madge's house to be accurate), I extricated myself from the car and waved goodbye as Sy tooted and sped off up the Ridgeway. Uncle Toby's white Jaguar was not parked out the front, and as I entered through the double garage access door, I pulled the cord to activate the fluorescent strip lighting. Only Aunt Madge's Mini was inside, Laurie's green Morris Minor was parked over to the side of the paved front garden, so both my uncle and Laurie were still at the police station, or out somewhere.

As I turned to close the garage door behind me, I saw something on the ground outside the door near the honeysuckle that vigorously climbed up the wall. The tin had a small dollop of bird dropping on it, so had been there some while for the sparrows that roosted in the greenery were well settled for the night.

A green and gold tin. Thinking that Aunt Madge might have dropped some of her shopping I picked it up. Lyle's Golden Syrup – treacle produced by Abram Lyle and sons, a delicious tin of sweet, caramelised flavour with a rich melt-in-the-mouth texture. Ooh, treacle on pancakes! It wasn't Pancake Day, that was long gone, but that sort of detail never perturbed Aunt Madge when it came to cooking something scrumptious. Or maybe she was planning on making treacle tart? That was as good. My mouth watered. I always associated Lyle with Tate and Lyle, but Abram Lyle had produced his famous syrup before merging with Henry Tate in the early 1900s, making their joint company responsible for refining something like 50% of the British sugar trade. I only knew this because I'd done a project at school about sugar. I won an end of term prize of a book token for it, which is probably why I remember the historical detail.

No wonder our teeth were succumbing to the need

for regular dental care. Mind you, sugar and poor dentistry had been a problem since Tudor times. The few teeth Queen Elizabeth I had by the time she'd grown old, were black and rotten. (I'd included that fact in my school project as well, along with a colourful drawing of Queen Bess and her blackened teeth.)

Aunt Madge was dishing up chicken pie and creamy mash. "Hello dear, I heard that Lotus roaring off, so knew you were home. Toby and Laurie will be late, so we'll eat without them."

I showed her the tin of treacle and told her where I'd found it.

"How odd," she said, frowning. "I haven't been shopping today, and it wasn't there this afternoon when I came back from doing the horses." My aunt owned two horses which were kept at a local livery yard. She employed a groom but rode every day when she could, and I always joined her on my days off or of an evening when the weather was co-operative.

"So no pancakes or treacle tart for dinner?" I said, disappointed, as she put my plate of dinner on the table.

"Sorry, no. Wash your hands and tuck in before it gets cold. I could do pancakes tomorrow if you like. But I'll buy a different tin, there's no knowing where that one has been or come from. I'll get Toby to have a look at it, just to be safe."

My mind went to one of Agatha Christie's novels where someone had been murdered by arsenic put into a pot of jam. Or was it strychnine in marmalade? Christie used poison a lot, a woman's weapon, or so it was widely believed. Christie also had extensive knowledge of poisons because she worked in a pharmacy during the first world war. But would someone seriously lace a tin of treacle with poison and leave it outside our garage for us to eat? Surely not?

More likely to be children playing tricks. Or my aunt didn't want to admit that she'd bought it, dropped it and forgotten about it!

Apart from the adornment by the sparrows, the tin didn't look like it was old or had been tampered with, but as a policeman's wife, Aunt Madge knew to be cautious about strange anomalies, so now that she'd pointed a possible danger out, perhaps she was right? Only would someone up to no good, or with a weird sense of humour leave a tin of treacle under a honeysuckle bush.

5

INTERLUDE: DS LAURIE WALKER

I only spoke to Jan briefly when I dropped DCI Christopher off at his home and swapped his car for mine. It was almost eleven and she was already in her pajamas so a brief kiss at the garage door. She could see that I was tired – it had been full on, looking for the lost girl and depressing that we'd come across not a single clue as to her whereabouts.

The first hour or so when looking for a child was always hopeful: gone off to a friend's house without asking, wandered to the shops – or the library. I've never forgotten my mum telling me about a time I'd 'gone missing' – funny when thinking back to it, but as it was happening, harrowing for Ma.

I'd been four years old and we were still living in a large Buckinghamshire town then. We'd moved to Devon a few years later. Mum had left me outside a toyshop while she went to the post office. Naturally, after a couple of minutes the lure of going *inside* outweighed peering in through the window.

Mum came back. No little boy outside the shop. She peeped inside. No little boy. Frantic she ran home: still no little boy. She ran back to the shops, to Dad's dismal and poky accountancy office that was situated above a fish and chip shop. Dad dropped everything, started the search again from the last known point of definition, the toyshop. He didn't quickly peep inside but went right in. I was happily helping the lady behind the counter place plastic farm animals in a glass display case. To this day I can't figure why Mum hadn't gone into the shop right from the start, even to ask if I'd been seen. The shopkeeper gave me one of the farm animals, a plastic donkey, for being such a good boy. Don't laugh, I've still got it somewhere.

No such easy outcome today, though. I felt guilty because I'd promised Jan I'd watch TV with her this evening – she was one of the rare people who had her own set in her own room – a cosy sitting room that her uncle and aunt had created from a spare bedroom. The privacy meant we could be together when we wanted, although Mrs Christopher, Madge, had made it quite plain that I was not to stay after midnight. I had hoped this would be relaxed once Jan and I had become engaged, but I suppose Madge only had our best interest at heart, protecting us from gossip and such. I could have forgiven any gossip tonight in exchange for some cosy comfort. We did manage to sneak the occasional intimacy together when opportunity arose, so I'm not complaining. Well, only a little.

Jan was a darling, she totally understood that I was shattered, she'd lived alongside a policeman's duties all her life, so knew what was what, and how important some of these things were. I intended to tell her that I would try to keep the weekend free, and see if I could take her to the circus that was setting up on Chingford Plain. Bartum's Circus arrived on the dot every year before Easter. Whitsun would see the fair arrive. Both were a headache for us cops as the crime rate shot up during those weeks – not from the circus or fairground folk, but from petty thieves who took advantage of the large crowds to pick more than a pocket or two.

I had the sinking feeling that I would not be able to keep a promise anyway. She mentioned the tin of treacle, and puzzling about that, I shoved aside any thought of making promises that I probably couldn't keep. The way things were going, the approaching weekend didn't look like it would be a relaxing one.

I was heading for home, my somewhat dismal digs at the section house. One of these days I might get a chance to start searching for a reasonably-priced flat, but money was tight and I was saving hard for our wedding. I got as far as Higham's Park Station level crossing, and had to wait for a train to chunter by. Then it stopped in the station, its last carriage slightly overlapping the crossing so the gates remained closed. By the time they opened I'd decided to turn round and have another look at the route Sally Armitage would have taken. Utterly pointless because it had been gone over with a fine-toothed comb already, but I knew I'd not sleep, despite being so tired. *Just one more look*, I told myself.

I parked near the school gates in what was really the back entrance beside a cul-de-sac in York Road, and got out, locked the car, my faithful Morris Minor. There was no one around – unlikely to be this time at night – and switching my torch on I proceeded up the narrow alley which led to Hall Lane and the library.

Trees provided quite a canopy, making the alley dark and even spooky. Traffic was passing ahead of me in Hall Lane, but not a sound from behind. Each side was high, wooden fencing. Had anyone called at the houses, I wondered? Searched the gardens? Of course they had, it would have been routine procedure. Besides, Sally couldn't have got into any of these gardens, she wasn't very tall and even I'd have found it difficult to climb over the fencing. I went back and started again, searching for any loose planks of wood or small holes that a child could have crawled through. Found nothing.

At the main road I crossed over, walked up the road a little way and turned left to the rose garden walkway that fronted the library entrance, stopping to shine my torch into the flower beds, even though I knew they'd been checked several times.

"You lookin' fer summink, mister?" The man's voice made me jump. I swung round, shone my torch full in his face.

"Oy! Leave it out!" he snarled, batting at the bright torch beam with his hands, "I ain't lookin' me best afta' a few tots o' whisky!"

That was an understatement. He looked like he hadn't shaved for over a week, needed a good wash, and smelled of, well, in addition to the whisky residue I'll just say that he stank. He was as sozzled as a sailor home on shore leave, and certainly needed to be put in the scuppers with the hosepipe on him.

"I'm looking for a little girl," I said, without thinking clearly.

"Ain't we all?" he cackled as he shuffled off. "Ain't we all?"

I was tempted to arrest him there and then, but truth to tell, I didn't fancy waiting around for a car, or escorting him to mine and forcing him into it.

Just as well I'd resisted temptation, for when I got back, I discovered that I had a puncture. I'd run over a broken bottle without realising and the passenger side tyre was as flat as a pancake. The only good thing, the night was clear and mild, so at least I didn't have to change a tyre in the pouring rain.

Puncture dealt with, I climbed wearily into the driver's seat and had to get out again to retrieve a flyer which was tucked under my windscreen wiper. I held it towards the nearest, somewhat feeble, street light to read the print. An advert for the circus. I stared at it for quite a while, realising that I had meant to make that promise about taking Jan to the Big Top. I'd forgotten. Hadn't said a word about it.

6

REVERSING THE POLARITY

The redecorating was going to be a nightmare. We opened to the public at ten of a morning and this would be a busy, but short, week for Friday the 20th was Good Friday and the library would be closed from Thursday evening right through until next Tuesday. I had an advantage, though, as I'd booked the following Tuesday off as leave, intending to spend some extra time with Laurie. So, adding in the normal Wednesday day off, I had six whole days of leisure to look forward to. Six delicious days of not having to get up for work, but until then, three days of the library open for readers eager to stock up on books. And the decorators to deal with.

We had the same every Easter, moaning that as we'd be closed Good Friday and Bank Holiday Monday we should not add the 'inconvenience' of also closing on the Saturday. The inconvenience for us, was the decorators. No hope of them doing anything over Easter, but we hoped that the normal closing day of this coming Wednesday would leave them to paint the ceiling above the counters where we took in and stamped out the books, an area that we couldn't move elsewhere or temporarily cover up.

Their intended 'early start' last Friday had helped once the start had finally been made. They'd spent most of Friday morning humming and hawing about the best place to begin, then decided, after carrying the ladders and canvas floor covering about for a while, to paint the ceiling above the children's and sound recording half of the library. To give the four men their due, once they *did* start, they quickly got on with it. After a tea break, that is.

That Monday morning, the bright new paint work looked lovely, but made the rest of the library look awfully shabby.

There was a queue of eleven people waiting outside for the library to open; we rarely had queues unless it was a special sporting day, like a football World Cup or the Grand National, in which case, except for a few non-sporty readers, the library was exceptionally busy all morning but emptied half-an-hour or so before the event was due to start. Sometimes there would be a mad dash afterwards – the National, for instance, for that finished before we were due to close at five on a Saturday, but the footie could go on for the entire afternoon, especially if it went to a penalty shoot out, or whatever the technical term is. So, to have a queue of people on a Monday morning was unusual. And, as it happened, annoying, although the difficulty was not their fault, but I do wonder about the intelligence of some people sometimes? Or lack of it. And decorators getting in the way of everyone, goes without saying.

Young Sally had not been found. No sign of her had come to light over the weekend. Her family must have been frantic, my heart went out to them even though I did not know them for they were not library members. Sally's disappearance had been mentioned on the morning news bulletins during BBC Radio 4's *Today* programme, so interest in her, at varying levels, had quickly spread. The topic of conversation on everyone's lips locally was the missing girl, and the library was proving to be an ideal meeting place to exchange speculative theories. Which would have been no problem were it not for the pots of paint, the labyrinth of ladders, cascading dust sheets, and four annoying interior decorators.

To be fair, Henry Jones was a decent boss. He got on with things – well they all did, once they'd actually started, but rather than begin in one of the quiet corners of the adult section, or near a less used non-fiction bay, they set up right in the middle, covering the romance and returned books shelves with their huge dust sheets, spreading more on the floor and propping up their long ladders. I'm not an expert at decorating techniques, but is it usual to start painting a high ceiling in the *middle* and then working outwards? Surely left to right or front to back would make more sense? Still, I suppose, as long as the job got done... After a first tea break they set to.

Naturally, after gossiping with us at the counter, the public headed for the shelves – the ones which were covered up. I mean, we have an entire library full of books, but you'd have thought the only books worth reading were those beneath the dust sheet covers.

Apparently people had no worries about getting covered by drips of paint from above, or brushing legs against paint pots. Those small facts didn't seem to bother our intrepid borrowers. A bee line was made for the dust sheets; one woman even contorted herself to duck under one of the ladders, causing it to rock precariously. The bellow which erupted from Joe atop the ladder was understandable, but not suitable language for a library. The lady, bright red with embarrassment, (or maybe indignant rage at being called what she had been called), scuttled out of the library without choosing more books. I wondered if she would come back or change to using North Chingford library instead.

Joe was in his late forties and was nice enough, but had a couple of annoying habits. One was a propensity to whistle tunelessly between his teeth, although he occasionally managed something vaguely recognisable. His co-workers called him Whiskers. His other habit was to use a version of East End Cockney rhyming slang of his own invention – or at least, no rhyming slang that I'd ever heard. I always thought that tea was 'Rosie Lee', for the stripper Gypsy Rose Lee. His variation was 'A cup o' North Sea'. With or without salt, I wondered?

Henry Jones, was also in his forties, and fairly jovial but with a preference for several tea breaks over actual work – oh sorry, *North Sea* breaks. I think he only had these because his three employees wanted them. A case of keeping them happy by keeping the kettle on.

Bill Edwards' nickname was Day-O. His habit, although not as annoying as Joe's tuneless whistling, was to say 'Day-O!' instead of hello or goodbye, or good morning or goodnight: Day-O as in the Calypso Banana Boat song, you know, where the singer, Harry Belafonte, sings *day-o, da-aa-ay-o*, and then sings about the morning daylight coming and wanting to go home. I usually remembered a later line about the highly deadly black tarantula. The first time I'd heard that song it put me off eating bananas for months. I remained not particularly fond of them.

The fourth one of the team was Adrian Blessit, he looked about thirty in age. His co-workers called him Adsy, and I wasn't sure if I liked or loathed him. He was very good looking, had a nice smile and was funny

– but was he *too* good looking, *too* smiley, *too* funny? He and Sy immediately didn't hit it off, probably because Adrian had managed to tip an entire load of returned music cassettes to the floor within seconds of Sy having sorted them out into order before putting them back in place on their revolving wooden racks in the sound recording part of the library. Sy had my sympathy. Cassette tapes were almost as good as vinyl for sound quality, were more practical, less expensive and took up less room, but they were a nightmare to handle as the plastic cases tended to slip and slide, so were forever being dropped. And the outer cases frequently cracked. Add to that, only two or three could be held at once so Sy used his cardboard box lid to sort and carry them. When Adrian knocked them to the floor, the thirty or so cassettes made quite a clatter.

In turn, I don't think Adrian appreciated being called a Winker. Only Sy didn't use the word 'winker'. His word was very similar, but I was naïve enough to not know what it meant, although had enough of an inkling to realise that it would not be a good idea to ask. (I was later glad I hadn't when I eventually found the original word in a dictionary.)

Another irritation after having to repeatedly tell the public to stay away from ladders and pots of paint, was me having to field questions about poor little Sally. I won't say that it was common knowledge that my uncle was a Detective Chief Inspector based at Chingford Police Station, but more than a few people seemed to be aware of the fact. Fortunately, less people knew that I was engaged to Uncle Toby's bagman, Detective Sergeant Laurie Walker, so I only had to politely answer questions with, "I'm sorry my uncle never discusses police business with me." The only other answer I gave was that to the best of my knowledge, no, Sally had not yet been found.

I rather wished that I hadn't been scheduled to work on the counter this Monday morning, but Mondays and Thursdays were my late shift nights which meant we were usually on the counter in the morning and in the office in the afternoon. This Monday, Gail and Millie kept me company. I liked both ladies. Gail was a few years older than me, full of fun and laughter, her bust was as large as her heart and her skirts were as short as our tea breaks. Pam was always ticking her off about it. Gail would switch to a trouser suit for a few days then go back to her short skirts. I must add, Gail never received any complaints from the public. Well, not the men at any rate. We did seem to get more men in during the evenings that she worked. Coincidence or not?

Millie – Millicent – was in her fifties and one of our part-timers. I think us younger staff often regarded her as a mother figure, the image helped along by the fact that she was always knitting things for her grandchildren… and for us. We had all received fabulous jumpers with intricate patterns for Christmas. I've no idea where she found the time to knit so prolifically.

During the morning, as efficiently as we could, we shelved the books that came in; when it was my turn for shelving, I had an armful of fiction, some of which I had to dump on the trolley as I was not prepared to scrabble around under the dust sheets and ladders. Adrian was down his ladder, replenishing his paint tray. Next to him, as yet uncovered, was the science fiction and fantasy section. Most fiction was shelved along the main bookcases in authors' surname order, but we had bays for popular subjects – romance, mystery and thrillers, westerns and sci-fi. It made shelving a lot easier and quicker, and suited the fans of those genres.

"So what's the difference between fairy tale fantasy and spacey tale science fictiony stuff?" Adrian asked, leering over my shoulder as I placed some books on the appropriate shelf, Ursula Le Guin, Arthur C. Clark and Tolkien's *The Lord of the Rings*.

"Fairy tale is about enchantment, where the currency is magic beans and the ladies wear long floaty dresses. Fantasy is where, if you're young you want to be Frodo or if you're old, you're content with Bilbo Baggins and a good book, and it's where the money is silver coin or elaborately engraved invisible rings. Sci-fi is about made-up ideas about science and space travel, where the currency is electronic credits and the ladies wear tight tops and leather mini skirts," I answered, rather cleverly, I thought. He didn't get the joke, Philistine that he was.

"Reading books is a waste of good drinking time," he sneered.

"*Not* reading books is a waste of what few cells are left in a mouldering brain." I was rather proud of that riposte as well. "Books are magic. They can take you anywhere, to any time, and because books are bigger on the inside than on the outside, every one of them is a Tardis in disguise."

Adrian sniffed disdainfully and cuffed his nose with his not-so-clean shirt sleeve. "What's a Tardis when it's at 'ome?"

I rolled my eyes and decided that Adrian had no soul. "Time And Relative Dimensions In Space. Dr Who's time-travelling machine."

"Who's he then?"

I was tempted to be precise and say Jon Pertwee, but decided to be more obtuse with this moron. "He's a Time Lord from Gallifrey, who can reverse the polarity of any neutron flow, whenever he needs to. And if he was here, he'd reverse the flow of that paint dripping off the end of your brush onto our nicely polished parquet floor." I walked away to the far end of the huge, central bookcase, leaving the gaffer, Henry Jones, to tear Adrian off a strip about the dripping paint and to get the mess he'd made cleared up.

I also heard Adrian say, "Stuck up bitch, that one." I guessed he meant me. I didn't mind too much; I'd rather be stuck up than ignorant. As Einstein once said, *Two things are infinite: the universe and human stupidity. Although I am not so sure about the universe.*

I adored science fiction. I had read nearly every book we stocked, and had a dream to write my own sci-fi best-seller one day. So far, I had fifty thousand words written towards my goal, with at least another thirty thousand to go. Which sounds optimistically positive until you take into account that I hadn't written a single word for over four months, leaving my poor hero, space smuggler Radger Knight, (rhyme it with badger), trapped inside a living alien matrix somewhere deep in an unexplored galaxy. Truth to tell, I had no idea how to get the poor guy out of his predicament. You would think that writing science fiction or fantasy would be easy because nearly all of it is made up, but the smallest factual details have to be believable in order for the rest of it to be plausible. Perhaps Radger ought to take a leaf out of Dr Who's book and simply reverse the polarity? It was a thought, except I had no idea what that one-off but very memorable script line actually meant. It was a good line, though. I wish I'd thought of it first.

I mused on that quote as I shoved the last book, a car repair manual, into its correct place at 629 in the Dewey Decimal System, and headed back to the counter where a small queue was building up. I knew most of the lines from every Dr Who as I always taped them on my tape recorder. It wasn't the same listening to only the words and the sound effects, but until someone invented visual TV recorders like they used on Star Trek, or I learnt efficient shorthand, this was the only method I had of repeating Dr Who. *A pity*, I thought, *that everyday problems can't be sorted by a simple reversal of time, let alone its polarity.*

I was thinking of poor Sally, who was probably dead by now. At least that was the general opinion, which, sadly, I privately agreed with. I would have liked to have asked Laurie, but I'd hardly seen him, or Uncle Toby, over the weekend. And when our paths had crossed, neither had wanted to talk shop.

7

TEA AND QUESTIONS

Another surprise came during the 4.30 tea break; Uncle Toby popped his head round the staff room door. His appearance was unusual. Laurie occasionally called by to say hello if he was in the area investigating criminals on his own, but this time my uncle was the one flying solo, driving his car himself – again unusual. Uncle Toby was a perfectly good and capable driver, but when on duty he preferred Laurie to drive so that he could read reports and files, or mull over a perplexing case. Or fall asleep, although he strongly denied that one.

"Laurie's working on something at the station," Uncle said as he nodded hello to the other staff. "I'm on my way there now, but I wondered," he reddened a bit and scratched at his nose, "a bit of an awkward cheek, but might I make use of your gents' convenience? Needs must and all that."

I set my book aside and jumped up from my chair, (a new novel started, *Jonathan Seagull* duly finished with great satisfaction), to show him where the 'facilities' were. I had to warn him about the paint tins. For some reason they had been stacked next to the handbasin in the gents' toilet. Why they weren't in the storeroom is anyone's guess, except Bert, our caretaker, porter, cum general handyman, had probably banned the paint because of the potential mess. It was good of him to be putting up with the ladders and other stuff, as his storeroom wasn't particularly large, and one entire wall contained shelving for books awaiting permanent disposal because of irreparable damage, or were books restricted from public view. (I often wondered whether Bert secretly read any of them.) The books which were to be destroyed were boxed up every so often and returned to Central Library where they, in turn, sent them to be repulped. Or at least, that's what I believed happened. I suspect, however, that they were simply tossed into an incinerator somewhere.

"I don't suppose there's any chance of a quick cup of tea?" Uncle Toby asked before he disappeared into the gents.

"I can offer some North Sea," I quipped, but he didn't hear. Just as well, really, as I would have had to explain the joke.

Looking very much relieved, he returned to the staff room and graciously accepted a chair and a mug of piping hot tea.

"Is there any news?" Gail asked, recrossing her legs and showing a good deal more thigh than she ought. Fortunately, Pam didn't notice.

"Nothing much, I'm afraid. A few parents saw her crossing the road – confirmed by the Lollipop Lady – but she seems to have vanished somewhere near the library."

He *harrumphed* a bit, a sure sign of indecision, again most unusual for my uncle. He took a breath. "We found her schoolbag and school clothes this morning, giving us reason to believe that she had come as far as the library."

Pam, Trish, Gail and I looked at each other. I could see in their faces that questions were wanting to be asked, but we knew better than to do so. Sy was the only one to speak.

"Her clothes? That doesn't sound too good. But there are lots of places where things not wanting to be found can be dumped or hidden in those alleys. They all have several empty garages, and back onto more than a few overgrown, neglected gardens."

Uncle Toby frowned at him over his mug of tea. "Know the alleys well, then, do you Mr Henbury-Clive?"

Sy smiled innocently, perhaps realising that he'd put his foot in a suspicious pile of do-do. "I use them, yes. It is much quicker to nip up through the alleys rather than go all the way round when I want to get to the shops. That overgrown cut-through alongside the rose garden outside leads to the flats opposite the cinema and Maynard's tobacconist. Saves me a good minute or two."

"*Mmm hmm,*" Uncle Toby nodded. "Does it? If you could pop into the police station sometime soon, we'd like to take your fingerprints. This evening or first thing tomorrow?"

Sy bridled with indignation. "Am I a suspect or something? I haven't seen, or touched, a schoolbag if that's what's worrying you Detective Inspector."

"Purely elimination purposes. If you haven't touched anything there's no need to worry. But we do need all the help we can get on this one, sir."

I knew my uncle. Sy was a suspect. I wondered why – how – they had concerns about him. I hoped it wasn't simply because Laurie didn't like him!

"Maynard's? Tobacconist? I didn't know you

smoked?" Trish questioned. I don't think she'd cottoned on to the nuances of the rest of the conversation.

"They sell other things apart from cigarettes, Trish. I'm rather partial to a quarter of their wine gums, and I do smoke occasionally," Sy answered with a tight smile. "The boys in the band smoke like chimneys, and I'm happy to clog up my lungs with tar when I'm with them."

"Cigarettes will ruin your singing voice," Pam advised.

Sy shrugged. "I only play guitar and add the occasional *la la* or *oo oo*. The guys don't let me sing, they claim that I sound like a donkey with a sore throat."

That, I didn't believe.

Uncle Toby drank his tea in between making small talk, then, about to bid farewell asked Sy another question as if he'd only just thought of it, which, of course, he hadn't. "I believe that's your red Lotus parked in Marmion Avenue?"

Sy nodded. "It is. Why?"

"Would you mind if I took a look inside?"

"Actually, yes I would." Because he had something to hide, or because of all the rubbish cluttering it up?

Uncle Toby pursed his lips. "Then perhaps you'd explain why you have several Polaroid photographs of little girls scattered on the front seat?"

I barely concealed my shock. Did Uncle Toby really suspect Sy of kidnapping Sally Armitage? Uncle Toby rarely made accusations unless he knew he could back them up by solid, factual proof. Photos of young girls? What photos? What was going on here?

With a bark of laughter, Sy threw back his head and slapped his thighs with his palms. "You're well and truly barking up a wrong tree Mr Christopher! They are photographs of my niece, Bethany-Anne, and her friends. Yesterday was her eighth birthday party, to which I and my younger brother were cordially invited. I gave her a Barbie doll, and rather regrettably, ate too much cake."

"We can verify that?"

"Yes, Detective Chief Inspector, you can."

"I can confirm that Sy told me that he had his brother staying with him and they were to drive back to Buckinghamshire together," I said.

"You met this brother?" my uncle asked. "Saw them drive off together?"

I went red. "Er, no, but Sy told me his intentions last Thursday."

"Not exactly a cast iron alibi," Uncle stated.

"I'll give you my mother and sister's telephone numbers," Sy offered. "They'll confirm that Barbie was dressed in a glamorous gold evening gown, and that I ate about a quarter of the cake. Victoria Sponge, by the way, with acres of pink and white butter icing. Very nice, but somewhat sickly when you eat too much of it."

Both men were being grittily pleasant to each other, although I could see the annoyance in Sy's eyes, and the doubt in my uncle's. Then he did a familiar sort of half-shrug where he pursed his lips and tipped his head to one side and I knew that all was well. Sy was no longer hovering on the edge of being arrested.

"If you could show me the photographs, just for the elimination record? I'd also advise putting them in an envelope or something, not leave them out for anyone to see. They might give a wrong impression? And maybe you would walk up this alley to the flats and the tobacconist with me? As you seem familiar with it maybe you'll spot something we have been unaware of?"

45

Sy sniffed, unsure, but consented after mentioning that our tea break was almost over, so he didn't have much time.

Pam interrupted. "Go with the Chief Inspector and take an extra five minutes when you return. I'm sure the rest of us can manage for a short while without you."

I went with them to the back, staff door.

It being nearly five o'clock. the decorators were finished for the day and were packing up. We had to wait while Joe and Adrian retracted one of their ladders and maneuvered it towards Bert's storeroom. I vaguely recognised the sort-of tune that Joe was attempting to whistle, but couldn't place exactly what it was. How he managed to keep the breathy noise up while carrying a heavy object is anyone's guess.

Uncle Toby was watching them intently. "It's Joe Kass, isn't it?" he asked.

Joe frowned. "What's that to you? Police harassment or something?"

My uncle shrugged. "You remember me as much as I remember you, then?"

"I remember. You caused the death of an innocent man."

"Not me personally. He was found guilty by a court of law, and he was responsible for his own actions."

"Pah! You coppers are all the same. Cheats and liars. You're happy to convict an innocent man in order to get an easy result."

"I'm sorry you think so, but that wasn't the case. He wasn't innocent. He held a young girl as hostage. Threatened to kill her, and others of the bank staff."

Joe thrust his face closer to my uncle and jabbed his shoulder with his finger. "I don't *think* so, I *know* so. Your lot pinned that robbery on him. He wasn't there."

Adrian set his end of the ladder down and inched

forward round it. "Leave it Uncle Joe. Water under the bridge."

Uncle? I hadn't realised that Adrian and Joe were related. Adrian's surname was Blessit.

"Cass?" I interrupted what could be turning into a nasty exchange with what I hoped would be an innocent question. "As in Mama Cass of the Mamas and Papas? I love her voice." I da-da-diddy-da'd a few lines about no one gettin' fat except Mama Cass from one of my favourite songs, *Creeque Alley*.

From behind me, Sy laughed. "No, her name is Cass Elliot, Cass with a C."

Joe snorted, begrudgingly. "I spell Kass with a K."

"From the Russian for cat?" Sy asked.

I frowned. How did he know these things? "Does that explain your nickname then, Joe? Whiskers? As in the cat's whiskers?"

My question, thank goodness, lightened the last hint of tension.

"Sort of, and your colleague's part right. Kass is Estonian, not Russian. My gran'pa were from Estonia, came to England in '17. Didn't like the Bolsheviks or the Germans. Or the corrupt police."

We all ignored that last, and I made a mental note to look up the history of Estonia when I had a chance.

Sy smiled at my uncle and gestured towards the open back door. "Shall we go, sir? I need to return to work."

Joe hefted the ladder into Bert's storage room and Adrian winked at me, but not in a pleasant fashion. "Skipping off early with your grandad are you, luv?" He grinned. "You'd better watch this one, Pops. She's an intellectual. More interested in books than a bit of 'ow's yer father."

Uncle raised an eyebrow. "I can't say that I mind such a quality in my niece. Intellect is preferable to ignorance." He nodded goodbye to me, and followed by Sy, went out of the open door.

Adrian pulled a face and I had to flatten myself against the wall to let him pass. "He your uncle then? A copper? That's interesting to know," he whispered as he deliberately squashed too close. "I like to go out with honest girls. They don't mess a bloke about."

I probably should have kept quiet but my rising irritation at his suggestiveness got the better of me. "He is Detective Chief Inspector Christopher, as your uncle clearly seems to already know," I stated contemptuously as I marched off to start the evening shift in the library.

Fortunately, the evening ahead promised to be decorator free, except everywhere was drenched in the smell of paint and turpentine, made worse now that the wind had changed direction outside and the main lobby doors had been closed, along with all the windows. The wind could blow a gale through the library when it came from the east, and become quite chilly, but as I walked into the library the smell of new paint suddenly hit me and everything started swirling. I staggered the three yards to the back door, desperate for some fresh air to clear my head. I heard Bert's distant, muffled voice as if he was talking in slow motion, and to my acute embarrassment I crumpled to the floor, flat out in a faint.

―――

Pam sat me down in a chair and gave me a glass of water to sip. Bert had run to summon my uncle, all of which seemed an enormous fuss but I truly did feel most peculiar. Uncle, when he arrived, a little breathless – he's not as young as he was – took one look at my chalk-white face and insisted that he'd leave

Sy in the care of a constable (who, I later learned, was keeping an eye on Sy's car), and was going to take me straight home.

I started to protest, but Pam agreed. The next thing I knew, I was in the passenger seat of Uncle's Jaguar and we were heading up Chingford Mount in the direction of Aunt Madge and home.

"I don't suppose you've got any mints, have you?" I asked. "My mouth is terribly dry, and I feel a bit queasy."

"Have a look in the glove compartment."

I did so, and found a small packet of Polos. There was also an unopened pack of rice. I wondered what it was doing there; Uncle Toby rarely did any shopping, he never had the time.

Noticing, he explained that it had been left on top of the car sometime during Saturday. "I'd forgotten all about it. I reckon someone at the station put it down, then walked off without it. I'll give it to the duty sergeant, see if he can find whose shopping was a little light."

I was only half listening; I felt terribly tired and disorientated. As soon as we reached home, my aunt bundled me off to bed with a cup of tea, a few digestive biscuits and a hot water bottle for my feet, not that I needed it, for my bedroom faced south west, so was warmed by the late afternoon sun. In addition, Poppy, one of our cats, had been catnapping on my bed all afternoon – where she stayed, determined not to be evicted.

I drank the tea, munched the biscuits, then snuggled down beneath the covers, my fingers absently stroking Poppy's chin, her purr lulling me to sleep.

Not that I needed much lulling, I went out like a light.

8

COWBOYS AND INDIANS?

I felt fine Tuesday morning, although Aunt Madge fussed, asking several times if I was *sure* I wanted to go into work. If it had been cold or wet I might have been tempted to stay tucked up in bed, but it was a beautiful spring morning, with the sun shining and birds singing their hearts out. Besides, there was nothing wrong with me. The paint smell had disagreed with me, and I'd probably not eaten enough on Monday afternoon. Aunt Madge ensured that I had a proper breakfast and then insisted on driving me to work, something she rarely did, even if the weather was awful.

I'd been brought up to believe that, unlike cricket, weather did not stop play. This came about because my aunt had horses and I'd had my own pony for several years – bless her, Rosie was retired by the time I started work at the library, but I'd graduated to riding Aunt Madge's horses by then anyway. Horses need doing whatever the weather, and although my aunt paid a groom to look after them, she insisted on riding every day, and naturally, if I wasn't working, I rode with her. Riding along the bridleways of Epping Forest on a pleasant evening was relaxing after a day's work.

Often, we simply trotted round the block, a distance of about five miles, but we went further afield together when we could. I always looked forward to the fresh air, especially when the sun shone, and a gallop across Chingford or Fairmead Plain was guaranteed to blow any lingering cobwebs away.

As tempting as the possibility of an extra, unexpected ride was – purely undertaken for health matters, you understand – if I missed work this Tuesday it would have caused a headache for my colleagues who would need to cover for me as it was the day I took books to the housebound. My responsibility to select books for my round, then deliver them along my set route with Harry driving the Waltham Forest Council van, was my responsibility. I liked visiting my ladies and gentlemen, although they were not all old, I must hastily add. 'Housebound' also meant disabled. One of my old gents was a particular dear, despite being stone deaf and having an obsession with watching westerns on TV. His brother had been murdered not long ago, so I kept an eye on the old chap. He seemed to be thriving now his grumpy brother was no longer there to bully him: it's an ill wind, as the saying goes.

Doing the route was tiring but there was no smelly paint and Harry always made sure that we stopped for a cup of tea and chunk of cake provided by the ladies who voluntarily organised afternoon teas in the Old Church Hall in aid of raising church funds, facts which I pointed out to Aunt Madge, so she had to agree with me about going to work. I didn't mention that the Book Delivery Service route would also mean I would not be bumping into Adrian or his coworkers too much. I wasn't quite certain what to make of Adrian, or what to do about him. Or did I need to do anything anyway?

I went across the paved front garden to open the

wrought iron gates while Aunt Madge backed the car out of the garage. There on the pavement was a toy Red Indian war bonnet, resplendent with what were supposed to be eagle feathers, although they looked more like goose quills to me.

I showed it to Aunt Madge.

"Oh, I expect it belongs to Mrs Johnson's two boys three doors down. I often hear them playing Cowboys and Indians in their back garden. I suspect they've dropped it. I'll pop it round to them later."

I shut and locked the garage doors while my aunt turned the car round and drove through the gates, waiting for me across the wide pavement. I closed the gates, climbed into the passenger seat and handed her the war bonnet. She scowled at it.

"No self-respecting native North American would be seen wearing goose feathers, and this looks homemade. Mrs Johnson is usually very good at making things, this doesn't seem to be her work at all. Maybe someone gave it to the boys? I wonder where the feathers came from?"

"There are wild geese on Connaught Waters and at Hollow Pond near Whipps Cross Hospital?" I suggested.

Aunt Madge poked at the thing for a moment then leant round to toss it onto the back seat. "Toby did say there's been quite a bit of poaching recently, but that was mostly foreign geese overwintering, and anyway, they would have flown away by now. These feathers are white, so domestic farm geese. I know the West of England breed is white and brown and the Embden is usually pure white, I've no idea of any others. I only remember being chased by an affronted Embden gander when I was courting with Toby." She laughed outright. "He came to my rescue, with one hand grabbed the goose by the neck, gave it a sound talking to, then before he released it, told me to run. Toby ran even faster!" She put the car into gear and joined the traffic on the main road. "I'll pick you up at five, shall I?" Then she asked, "Are you seeing Laurie this evening?"

I sighed rather glumly. "No. I've only seen him briefly since last week. I was hoping to go to the circus with him tomorrow, but I doubt that's to happen now, he's not even mentioned it."

"It's not his fault dear, this missing girl is taking a toll on everyone."

"I know, but... well, just but."

"It's what we have to learn to live with if we're married – or in your case, engaged – to a policeman. And he did send you those lovely flowers last night, which was thoughtful of him."

I smiled. "It was, although I was fast asleep so didn't know they were there until I woke up this morning, and maybe he shouldn't have sent chrysanthemums? Aren't they associated with funerals?"

Aunt Madge frowned as she braked to avoid a bus that had pulled out without checking what was coming up behind him – our car. "Don't men ever use their mirrors?" she muttered, then returned to our line of conversation. "Unlike the Victorians, modern men don't always understand the language of flowers, but chrysanthemums can mean different things to different cultures. In East Asia, China and Korea for example, they are supposed to ward off evil spirits and bring longevity in the afterlife."

I giggled. "I guess you're a long time in a grave!"

"Chrysanths represent death and grief in Japan, so much so that they are on the Imperial Seal and often feature on Japanese gravestones. But in the west, we associate them with celebration: weddings, anniversaries and birthdays, for instance. Besides, they have some beautiful colours and they last quite a long time."

"Roses would have been nice, though."

Aunt Madge wagged a finger at me. "Roses are expensive, and be grateful for what you did get. Although a bunch of daffodils would have been a good choice. Do you want any shopping? I've got to get a few bits after dropping you off; lamb chops from the butcher and maybe some hot-cross-buns from the baker for afters?"

"And something from the candlestick maker?" I laughed. "Butcher, baker, candlestick maker?"

"Actually, that's an idea. There's a new range of lavender scented candles in Boots. I had some for Christmas, used the last one the other week. Soaking in a lovely hot bath, candles for light and Radio 3 playing... ah, bliss!"

She didn't mind foul weather, but also loved her cosy homey comforts, did my wonderful aunt.

9

CIRCUS TRICKS

As it turned out, Gail, Trish and Clara at the library also wanted to see the circus, so we arranged that the four of us would go together for the Wednesday evening performance. Wednesdays were our day off as the library was closed, so we had time for ourselves during the day and something to look forward to come the evening. I was surprised when Sy, overhearing us talking, said he'd like to come with us. I was surprised that circuses would be his 'thing', but he, slightly red-faced, admitted that he'd never been to a live circus. "Not the sort of thing my mother would class as suitable entertainment."

I hoped I'd never have to meet his mother, she sounded awful. I wondered what she thought about her son being in a band – decided that she probably thought he meant band as in orchestra.

We met in the lounge bar of the Royal Forest public house where Sy bought us all a drink; he had beer, us girls opted for shandy. Seated at a table he showed us the photographs that my uncle had been concerned about.

"It seems that because I was stupid enough to leave

them out in full view, someone local had seen them, realised they were of little girls and put two and two together to make ninety-six. They'd reported the car and the photos to the police."

They were definitely of a children's party, and one photo of Sy with butter icing smudged all round his face was going to be a future good teasing subject. He even had some in his hair, what had he been doing with it!

"Mama confirmed I was at the party, and so the photos are of a genuine subject matter, nothing sinister about them. And I provided my fingerprints this morning, so I'm clear as far as that schoolbag goes. And the Albert Café has confirmed that I was there chatting for quite a while, so I'm innocent as far as this business about Sally is concerned. I hope," he told us. "That schoolbag has been confirmed as hers, but there was only a pencil case and a schoolbook with her name on it in it. Her teacher has said that there must have been other things, because she remembers seeing another bulging bag inside during the day."

Between us we puzzled about the information, but came up with no viable solution so, drinks finished, walked, arm in arm, down the hill to where the red and white striped Big Top had been erected at the edge of the Plains. Aunt Madge and I had ridden across there in the morning, our horses acting silly when they saw the four elephants secured in a fenced-off area. The lions roaring in their cages didn't seem to bother the horses at all, but the elephants – you'd have thought they were abominable equine-eating space monsters or something. It's amazing how much snorting and cavorting a horse can do in the space of about two yards. The circus horses were in another fenced off area, contentedly grazing and seemingly oblivious of the elephants and the jungle roars of the big cats. I was looking forward to seeing those horses perform, but not the elephants or the lions. Wild animals, I believe, ought to stay in the wild or at least as near to the wild as possible. On a coach trip with the Girl Guides, I'd been to Longleat Safari Park soon after it had opened in 1966, and found it wonderful to see the animals in an environment that was as near as possible to their natural habitat.

The only other non-domestic animals to perform were a troop of chimpanzees, although Sy insisted that the collective name was a 'whoop'. He could be a bit of a know-it-all bore at times. I was tempted to remind him about his Muslim faux pas to pull him down a peg or two, but it would have embarrassed him in front of the others.

The monkeys were fun, but I'm not a monkey fan and their act did rather copy the amusing Mr Piano Shifter TV tea commercial of them messing about with a piano. It was fairly obvious that the piano itself was one of those automatic cylinder ones, for there was no way the chimps could have played such jolly tunes – equally obvious that it was also on well-oiled rollers for them to have pushed it around so easily. Even so, the act was funny.

I'm not a clown person either as I'm not keen on slapstick comedy. I did laugh when we thought one clown with an enormous orange wig was about to throw a bucket of water over us... it turned out to be confetti. (I even found some in my bra that night when I eventually got home. It must have worked its way down my neck.)

Oh dear, I'm making this sound like I didn't enjoy the evening, which isn't, mostly, accurate! Let me start again.

I wouldn't say no to a ride on an elephant if I'm ever offered one, their performance was the usual stuff, but I couldn't help feeling sorry for them. I don't mind Indian elephants working, lifting and carrying logs and such, but being made to perform senseless and humiliating circus tricks is different. I'm too influenced by Disney's *Dumbo*, I think. The only thing I remember about that film was sobbing all the way through it.

The performing dogs were entertaining, toy poodles and some other fluffy breed, Pomeranian, I think. Their tricks were very clever, and let's face it, little dogs are natural at performing tricks, so nothing to complain about there.

After the dogs, the horses were *gorgeous*. There were three equine acts, two before the interval, and one after. A lady riding side-saddle did a very impressive performance, showing various movements and proving that anything you could do riding astride could be done equally well aside – including jumping what, to me, looked like a very high fence, but I think it was only about three-feet really. Then a troop of eight Cossack riders entertained us, although I wouldn't mind betting that they hadn't come from anywhere near Russia. Their acrobatics were incredibly skilled, especially as their act was undertaken in the circus ring which wasn't a very large arena.

The effect was slightly marred by Sy whispering to me, "Bet you can't do any of that on your old nags?"

I'm not sure if I was more insulted by his lack of faith in my riding ability or him calling my aunt's two wonderful horses 'old nags'. OK, no, I couldn't do any of those bareback riding stunts, and had no intention to try, but that isn't the point is it?

I also, somewhat to my surprise, enjoyed the high-wire act; how they balanced on stools and chairs on a thin line of wire above the ring with no safety net… or why risk the danger, come to that, I'll not understand. When the lights went up for the interval the arena party started erecting a circular metal cage, so we guessed the lions would open the next half. I'd drawn the short straw to buy tubs of ice creams for everyone, and was slightly disconcerted to discover Adrian Blessit, the painter and decorator, standing in the queue. He beckoned for me to join him. I was hesitant because I didn't know if I liked him or not, but he was near the front, I would have to go to the back.

"Bit tame, some of these acts," he said as I joined him.

"I doubt you could do many of those tricks!" I retorted. "Performers make it all look easy, but I bet it isn't."

He didn't answer, but as we moved up one in the queue he said, "Fancy going for a drink after?"

Really? He was asking me out? "No thank you, I'm here with friends."

"They can come too."

"No thank you." Apart from the fact that I was engaged to Laurie – although maybe he didn't know that? – he was ten years older than me. And not my type.

"Your copper boyfriend wouldn't like you enjoying yourself, I suppose."

"My fiancé, not my boyfriend. He has no objection whatsoever about me enjoying myself but he happens to be working this evening."

"Locking up innocents?"

"No, searching for a missing girl. But anyway, we're all going for a meal when this has finished." I mentally kicked myself. What if he asked to come too?

I was saved any further embarrassment by it being our turn at the kiosk. Adrian bought one ice cream for himself, while I selected what I wanted and paid. Clutching five very cold tubs, I started to head back towards our seats but he insisted on being helpful and took three of the tubs from me. We walked up the narrow, stepped aisle to the third row where the others were sitting. He smiled pleasantly, handed out the tubs, gave a small sort of bow and disappeared further up the aisle. I lost track of where he went for the lights went down.

"Fancy him being here!" Trish gushed. "Is he with someone do you know? He's rather dishy, isn't he?"

I guess he was good looking, but I replied that I didn't know if he was here on his own or not, and concentrated on trying to scoop solid ice cream with a tiny wooden spoon.

Following the lions (not too bad an act, but I did wonder if they were sedated), came the trapeze artists. As with all the performers, they were exquisite in their sequined, sparkly costumes and were breathtaking to watch. If one of them had missed their timing and not caught the hands of the other as she or he flew through the air… Goodness, it doesn't bear thinking about! A mock camel race came next and it wasn't particularly good, but I haven't much enthusiasm for camels. They smell and they spit. I rode one in Tangier where Aunt Madge, Uncle Toby and I went on holiday in 1967 when I was fourteen. Be warned, if ever you ride a camel you mount while they are 'sitting' down, and they get up in three lurching stages. Believe me, you'll feel seasick. I also remember being embarrassed by Uncle Toby on that holiday. Every time we ordered a drink he asked for Coca Cola. I kept telling him that we usually called it 'Coke', but he persistently ignored me. Oh, the daft things that bother young teenagers!

A lady in a very sparkly costume entered the circular arena with her five bay and five grey (white to non-horsey people), liberty horses, which were superbly trained, although their performance was basically only dressage without a rider, dressage being the equivalent of horses dancing. Rubbish if I tried it, as I hadn't the patience to practise but incredible when watching the professionals. Dressage was originally far more sinister than anything that could be classified as equine ballet, for in Medieval times the movements were designed as accomplished training for horse and rider in the melee of the battlefield. The horses were an additional weapon – defensive and offensive. To strike out with front hooves, kick back, move sideways, pivot on the spot, all were movements that could get the rider instantly out of trouble. You wouldn't think that something so beautiful to watch could evolve from something so violent, would you?

A troupe of dwarfs finished the show with some highly amusing antics intertwined with incredible acrobatics. The theme was the nursery rhyme *There was an old woman who lived in a shoe*. The lights went down and an enormous old boot was wheeled in; suddenly a door and windows were flung open and twenty 'children' came tumbling out, followed by an acrobat dressed as the old woman. I say children, for they were all dwarfs, dressed as children. According to the programme, they were all one family, mum, dad, sons, daughters, aunts, uncles and cousins.

The boot swung open into two halves so the audience could see that inside it was a sort of cramped house, with a living room and mock kitchen downstairs, and beds upstairs (except there weren't any stairs). The act was great fun, for the old lady was trying to get everyone to bed, but none of her 'children' wanted to go, so as soon as she'd chased some to the upstairs (via various clever acrobatics), they whizzed out the other side sliding down ropes or tumbling down onto piles of straw. Throughout, the circus orchestra was playing various nursery rhyme tunes, which, before long, we were all singing along to.

Hickory Dickory Dock, Polly Put the Kettle On, Insy Winsy Spider, Pop Goes the Weasel, Sing a Song of Sixpence.

One of the females, dressed in huge, fluffy pink pajamas and with masses of blonde, curly hair tied up in old-fashioned curling rags (obviously a wig), stood at the edge of the ring encouraging the sing-song by mock-conducting us, until the old woman pretended to tell her off. The girl grinned and waved directly at us before the old woman chased her off with one of those old fashioned witches' brooms. Of course, we enthusiastically waved back at her.

I was thrilled when my favourite song, an apparent nonsense verse, was included as a finale. It makes perfect sense when sung or spoken aloud, but is otherwise ridiculous:

Mairzy doats and dozy doats and liddle lamzy divey. A kiddley divey too, wouldn't you?

If the words sound queer, sing it slower: *Mares eat oats and does eat oats and little lambs eat ivy. A kid'll eat ivy, too; wouldn't you?*

I'm not a very good singer, but I warbled along to this last song at the top of my voice. It's amazing how the rhymes we grew up with come so easily to mind as soon as you hear the tunes again isn't it?

The entire audience was in stitches throughout the act, the only thing to mar it was the people sitting behind us who made disparaging remarks about the dwarfs, calling them stunted midgets, which was insulting and out of order. Part of my anger might have been because of my own inappropriate insensitivity the other day when I'd made that silly remark to poor Sally Armitage.

The final parade was even more spectacular than the rest of the show, with all the performers, including three horses with some of the performing dogs riding them, and one of the elephants carrying some of the dwarfs in one of those elephant canopy-covered houses – are they called howdahs? This too was covered in sparkles and glittery fringes. Two of the chimps, holding hands with their trainer, entered dressed in party frocks, while the clowns went around the edge of the arena tossing sweets to the children in the audience. (Sy caught one and promptly ate it.)

What was also nice, quite a few of the 'background' workers came in to take a bow as well: the grooms and animal supervisors, the costume designers, hair and makeup people, the lighting manager, the stage managers and general roustabouts, all giving an idea of the roles and responsibilities that, when combined, create the magic that is the wonder of the circus.

We left the Big Top, feeling suitably entertained, except, too much popcorn, candy floss and then the ice cream (and the sweet), hadn't gone down too well with Sy. He was dreadfully sick on the way back to the car park where he'd left his car. Serve him right for overstuffing himself with too much sugary food. He insisted he was all right, so us girls left him to drive himself home, and went towards the bright lights of Station Road in search of somewhere to partake of a nice meal. (I suppose I'd better add that Sy *was* fine once he'd thrown up, otherwise we would not have abandoned him.)

Chasneys, a rather swanky restaurant, was still open for service, and we managed to get a table near the window. Despite the ice cream (and some popcorn), I was hungry and tucked into a rare treat of Steak Diane, followed by Black Forest Gateau. Washed down by a glass of house red wine.

The only thing that spoiled the entire evening: Adrian Blessit was waiting at the bus stop.

10

A FRIGHT IN THE NIGHT

My colleagues all lived in South Chingford, or beyond in the next town along, Walthamstow, but I lived only about a ten- or fifteen-minute walk away, so it wasn't worth me getting a bus, plus, being rather stuffed full from Chasneys I thought a walk would be better for my digestion. I agreed to wait at the bus stop with the girls as it would have made the end of an enjoyable evening fall flat if I'd merely left them, so we crossed the main road arm in arm, and giggling rather a lot. (Helped along by the wine we'd shared.) There, sitting in the bus shelter was Adrian, smoking a cigarette. I think he'd had several because there was quite a pile of cigarette butts and ash by his feet. Had he been waiting for us?

"Evenin'," he said with a slight nod and a cheesy grin. "You all look like you've had a good time."

"We have," Trish smiled back at him. I again had the impression that she liked him – rather her than me, she was welcome to him. Trish was in her mid-twenties with no boyfriend at present, and from what I gathered, had a list of exes behind her.

"You catching the bus, too?" Adrian said to none of

us in particular, although he seemed to be looking more at me than the others. I didn't answer. Trish told him where we all lived – in general, that is, not specifically. I think she was about to say that I was intending to walk, but I interrupted.

"Did you enjoy the circus?" I asked him.

"It was OK. Seen better, seen worse. Nice seeing the ladies in those skimpy costumes though. I bet you look good in a bikini?"

I don't think any of us knew to whom he was referring, so there came an awkward silence. Fortunately we could see the bus coming, so we shuffled to the edge of the kerb, ready to board the red 69 Routemaster. Acting the gentleman, (I had my doubts about this being his true nature), Adrian stepped aside to allow my friends to board, then stepped onto the bus's open platform himself, grinning at me and giving a cocky salute. I ignored him and waved goodbye to the girls as the bus rolled away.

As the traffic was fairly quiet, I didn't bother walking to the zebra crossing but crossed the road from where I was, and once past the row of houses, strolled along The Parade where there were some interesting shops. Most of them, naturally at this time of night, (not far off 10.30), were closed, but one or two had their window lights on to display various wares. I had a quick peek in Brimble's window. His was my favourite shop in North Chingford, a bookshop and stationers owned by avid photographer, James Brimble. Mr Brimble had achieved quite a bit of fame – and not just local – with the publication of his wonderful book about Epping Forest, which not only included stunning photographs and an interesting history of the entire forest, but also had a set of detailed maps. I'd spoken to Mr Brimble several times, in his shop and while I was out riding, a very kind and generous gentleman who held a deep passion for both his hobbies. My signed copy of his book is one of my special treasures.

I lingered a while, taking note of a couple of books that looked tempting, then walked on. There were a few people about, couples mostly, going home from the pub, (I assumed), for most were coming from the direction of the Bull and Crown at the end of Station Road, opposite the parish church.

It was longer to walk round the church via the main road, so I took the shorter route past the library – North Chingford library was more modern than 'my' one in South Chingford, but I don't think it had as much charm or personality. It *was* warmer in winter, though! Adjoining the library was Chingford Assembly Hall, where I'd attended several various events with my uncle and aunt. These sort of public functions were expected of him, given his position as a DCI. I appreciated the dinner part of the dinner and dances, but not the dance bit; Aunt Madge always enjoyed herself, which was fair enough. Being a previous debutante she was a pretty good ballroom dancer. Uncle Toby wasn't too bad either, although he preferred a waltz rather than a quickstep or foxtrot.

I did wonder whether I'd made the right choice as this shorter route behind the church wasn't well lit. Near the church hall, where Aunt Madge went for her Townswomen's Guild meetings, the shadows became even deeper and darker. I stopped to listen. Were those footsteps I could hear behind me? Or was I imagining it? I could hear the traffic on the main road, and the church bells struck the half-hour. Laughter drifting from the Bull and Crown, the wind rustling in the trees lining the alley ahead. Nothing else. I walked on. Then I heard a cough and a hand grabbed my arm.

I screamed.

11

THE WALK HOME

"Whoa! Shush, it's only me!"

I dragged my arm free and turned in fury to face Adrian Blessit.

"You scared the life out of me!" I shouted. If I hadn't been shaking so much, I think I would have hit him.

"Thought you'd appreciate an escort after all," he grumbled.

"Not one that sneaks up behind me in the dark, I don't!"

He shrugged, muttered an apology.

From somewhere nearby a man called out. "You all right miss? Do you need assistance?" He must have heard my scream.

I called back. "No, but thank you – my friend startled me, that's all!"

In the dim streetlighting I could see that Adrian was grinning. "Ah, so I'm a friend now, am I? Glad to hear it."

I snorted in what I considered to be contempt, and continued walking. He fell into step beside me.

I said nothing for several yards, then ventured, "I thought you were on the bus."

"I was. I hopped off at the next stop before the conductor came to take a fare."

"And followed me."

"Yes. I didn't think a pretty girl like you should be walking home alone."

I was flattered. And he was probably right – about the walking home. I considered myself rather plain, not pretty.

We waited for the lights to turn red and the traffic to stop, then crossed the road.

Behind us was the police station, an old Victorian house awaiting demolition and a new, modern, replacement built instead. I half wondered if perhaps I ought to call in, ask if Uncle Toby or Laurie were still around. Then I told myself that I was being silly. I didn't have far to walk. This was a fairly busy main road. There were other people about, and anyway, did I have anything to fear from a painter and decorator who seemed to fancy me? OK, yes, I *was* flattered.

As we walked, Adrian – I couldn't bring myself to use his workmates' nickname of Adsy – had his fingers thrust into his tight jeans' front pockets and was whistling beneath his breath.

"You need to be careful," I warned, "you whistle just the same as Joe. Tuneless and annoying."

He guffawed. "Rubbed off on me, I guess. And it wasn't tuneless, I was whistling *Ride a Cockhorse,* the kiddies' rhyme."

"Why that one in particular?" I laughed. "We sang quite a few at the circus."

"Aye, that act were good fun, weren't it?" He jerked a thumb over his shoulder, indicating behind us. "That song because over there is a Banbury Cross."

"The war memorial? Chingford Cenotaph isn't a cross as such."

"And you could easily be a fine lady on a white horse."

"Except I haven't got a white horse, my aunt's horse is a grey dun. Nor do I have rings on my fingers or bells on my toes."

"No idea what a grey dun is, love. And you have, you've got a sparkly engagement ring given to you by that boring weasel and pop who's as up himself as a ferret in a hen house."

There was nothing I could say to that, so we walked on in silence. Perhaps I should have defended Laurie? He wasn't boring, nor was he 'up himself', although I wasn't certain what Adrian actually meant. Laurie wasn't arrogant or smug. He was just conscientious about – and good at – his job.

Maybe a little *too* conscientious?

I gave up, had to ask. "Weasel and pop? You've lost me."

"Cockney slang for a cop. Surely, you've heard that before?"

I shook my head. It was a new one on me.

"Cigarette?" Adrian offered, digging into his leather jacket pocket.

"No thanks, I don't smoke. Never have, don't intend to start."

He paused to light one for himself. I continued walking, at a slightly brisker pace, but he easily caught me up.

"Do you like honeycomb?" he asked, thrusting a bar of Crunchie at me.

"Oh! I love Crunchie, my favourite chocolate bar." I couldn't help myself. I eagerly took the offering.

"Can't stand it," Adrian said. "Uncle Joe gave it me earlier. Silly sod knows I'm not keen."

I unwrapped it and took a bite, sucked the

chocolate and let the honeycomb melt in my mouth. Delicious! "A Crunchie bar is mentioned in Enid Bagnold's novel *National Velvet*," I said, before taking another bite. "I think that's why I love it, Velvet Brown's choice of chocolate, therefore Elizabeth Taylor's."

"Eh?"

"You must know who Elizabeth Taylor is!"

"Of course I do, but what's the connection?"

"It was one of her first starring roles when she was only twelve years old playing Velvet – Grand National Velvet in the film."

"Oh. I see. I think."

It didn't take me long to eat the whole bar. I licked the melted chocolate off my fingers and stuffed the empty wrapper into my coat pocket. "I'm not sure if the film had the Crunchie bar though. It might have only been in the book."

"I don't read books. Only snobs read books."

I ignored the snob bit, had already gathered that he didn't read. I couldn't understand people who didn't. What poor, unenriched lives they must lead?

"So, the old guy's a copper, eh? Your uncle?"

"He isn't old and yes, he's a policeman and my uncle. I was orphaned when I was little."

His turn not to say anything for a few minutes. Then, "Yeah, I know, Uncle Joe told me about you and your dad. Back in the autumn of '58 your uncle arrested Uncle Joe's brother-in-law on a trumped-up charge of armed robbery. He went to prison. Hanged himself in his cell."

1958. That was the year my father had been murdered. I was five and remember almost nothing about it. I'd blocked the trauma from my mind. Mum had died a few months later, I had no idea why or how, no one had ever told me, and I had never asked.

"Uncle Joe's only sister was my mum," Adrian said.

I had to work that out for a moment before I understood the implication. "Oh. The brother-in-law was your dad?"

"*Mm.* Mum died of cancer a year later. Uncle Joe brought me up." He gave a small laugh. "I was fifteen when Dad died, so that makes me and you orphans. We have something in common already, darlin'."

Being an orphan? Not exactly a good thing to share. I pondered whether I ought to defend Uncle Toby's reputation, but recalled that he'd done so himself quite adequately when Joe Kass had confronted him. I opted for a different tack. "You seem fond of your uncle. Did he get you the job as a painter?"

"He did. He's known Henry a long time. Dad, Joe and him were squaddies together during the war. Before they were demobbed, they planned to start a business together. The decorating thing turned up, but Dad and Uncle Joe didn't have the money to buy the previous owner out, so Henry bought it by himself. He's done all right since, an' always been happy to employ me and Joe. Uncle Joe reckons that seeing as Henry ain't got no kids he might pass the business on to me when he retires. After all, it should have been ours in the first place."

"That'll be nice for you."

"I'll be well off. Henry has a big house at Woodford Green, and a holiday cottage up at Jaywick. One day they'll be mine."

Was he trying to impress?

We were well along the Ridgeway, when suddenly there came a burst of activity from the fire station opposite us on the corner of College Gardens. Blue lights were flashing, men were darting about and the station doors flung open. With a clamour of bells the fire engine burst out, the traffic stopped and the firemen were off at full speed.

"I hope it's not the library on fire!" I laughed, a little breathless. Seeing a fire engine called out on a shout was always exciting.

Before long we had reached the junction with Endlebury, and as home was on the other side of the main road I had to cross over. I stopped walking, realised that I should have asked where he lived ages ago. What if he was now out of his way?

To my belated asking he shrugged. "I share a house with Uncle Joe near Walthamstow High Street. No point in getting my own place. Too expensive. I'd like something nice near here one day, though."

I ignored the second bit. "Oh, if you need Walthamstow, you'd better stay on this side of the road to wait for the next bus." I pointed to the stop that was a few yards ahead of us, then pointed to the houses opposite. "I live over there. Thanks for the company, I appreciate it. And sorry I screamed."

He chuckled. "Under the circumstances I expect I'd've screamed as well."

"Oh, look," I cried, "there's a bus coming now. Stick your arm out, this is a request stop."

He grabbed my hand and pulled me behind him to run to the bus stop, his other arm outstretched and waggling as if it were a demented windmill sail.

The bus pulled to a halt with a squeak of brakes, its interior lights bright and a few people aboard. I could see the conductor inside, towards the front peering out at the stop, his arm reaching up, ready to flick the cord and ring the bell to alert the driver to move off again as soon as the new passenger was aboard.

I expected Adrian to immediately jump onto the bus's open platform, but he didn't. He bent forward and kissed me. On the mouth.

"See you t'morrer'!" he called as he leapt onto the bus and waved at me while hanging on to the pole, leaning out slightly as the bus picked up speed.

I didn't know whether to wave back or not. I was somewhat confused, I wasn't sure if I was secretly pleased at that unexpected kiss, or outright indignant.

12

A SILLY TIFF

To my surprise, (it seemed an evening of surprises!) Laurie opened the front door as I approached, the security lights having come on to alert him. It shouldn't have been a surprise as such, because his car was still parked outside, but somehow I just assumed that he was working late. After all, that's why he hadn't come to the circus with us. And why I practically hadn't seen him all week. I didn't expect to find him waiting for me at home.

Had he seen Adrian walking with me? More important, had he seen him kiss me? To my shame I pushed past Laurie into the house, not offering my cheek for a kiss or even saying anything nice. Instead, I grumbled.

"What are you doing here? I thought you were working late again?" I slid my coat off and hung it on the newel post at the bottom of the stairs. I noticed a vase of tulips on the telephone table and bent to sniff at them. Aunt Madge always managed to arrange flowers elegantly. Me, I dumped any bunch of flowers in water and that was that.

"The DCI was tired and there's nothing more we

can do, so we shut up shop for the night. They've gone up to bed. I said I'd wait to ensure you got home safe. I've missed you, sweetheart."

"Well I've been here, and I'm grown up enough to take care of myself. It's not even eleven yet! Want a cup of tea or coffee? Cocoa? I'll be off to bed myself soon, it's been a busy day." I went into the kitchen, flicked on the lights and bent to stroke Poppy who was curling herself around my legs hoping for an extra feed. I put the kettle on and fiddled with fetching mugs from the cupboard.

"The circus was good," I said. "I loved the horses." Basil, our other cat, jumped in through the cat flap. Supposedly, cats which push cautiously through a cat flap are quiet and timid. Those which have no regard for them are bold and like to think of themselves as the boss. That definitely summed Basil up. He sniffed at his food bowl, finding it empty, glared disgusted at me and promptly returned outside again, his black, sinuous body disappearing through the flap like a sort of magician's trick.

Should I mention Adrian, or should I keep quiet?

"Did you get the bus with the others?" Laurie asked. "I saw the bus drive off."

Oh blimey! Then it occurred to me: Adrian had kissed me literally as he'd jumped on board, so we were *behind* the bus and he would have been out of sight. Laurie couldn't possibly have seen – and he assumed I'd got *off* the bus, not that someone with me was getting *on* it. I'm not one to lie; being the ward of a conscientious policeman who very much valued the necessity for truth, that's how I'd been brought up. But sometimes the truth can have dire consequences. So better to not lie – but not utter the truth either. Keeping quiet was often a good compromise.

"The conductor was in a hurry to move off," I said,

"I expect it's his last shift and he didn't want to waste any time. Left me quite breathless!"

"I won't have tea or anything," Laurie said as the kettle started to boil, "I'm knackered, could do with a good night's sleep. Look, I'm sorry I've not been much fun this week, this missing girl, it's been hard, always is when kiddies are involved, especially when as each day passes, it's more likely that she's dead."

Oh, he looked so shattered! Dark circles were visible beneath his eyes, his skin pale, his cheeks hollow. I felt thoroughly ashamed of myself! I flung my arms round him, buried my head in his chest and muttered a half-choked apology.

Laurie stroked my hair then kissed the top of my head. "Don't be silly, you've nothing to apologise for, you've had a rotten week too. How are you now, after that funny turn the other day?"

I'd almost forgotten about it. "I'm fine. I think it was the sudden smell of paint. It isn't an odour that sits well with me, it often makes me feel sick."

"And you've got those decorators in at the library all week? Oh poor you."

"It should be OK, I've got a couple of extra days off next week after the Easter holiday – nearly an entire week off in all, with any luck they'll be finished and gone by the time I go back."

Laurie looked suddenly sheepish.

"You've forgotten, haven't you?" I said pulling away from him and putting my fists on my hips.

"Er. Yes. Sorry."

"We were going to go out for daytrips. I was looking forward to going to that Newmarket stud to see the foals. And we were going to go to Kew Gardens, and…"

"Harry and Pete wanted to take leave, they have kids and I…"

"And you gave up your booked leave so they could take theirs."

His sheepish expression deepened. "Er, no, I forgot to book it in the first place. I've been busy, you know I have."

I switched the kettle off. Walked out of the kitchen, turning the lights off as I went.

"I'm going to bed. Make sure the latch is down on the front door to lock it when you leave."

13

INTERLUDE: DS LAURIE WALKER

I stood in the dark kitchen for a few minutes, perfectly aware that I was an absolute arse, but as aware that there was something Jan was holding back from me. Something she wasn't saying. Fine detective I was! I hadn't a clue what, nor what to do about it.

To be fair, there was something I was keeping secret too, something that, on reflection, maybe she should know but it wasn't my place to tell her. Both DCI Christopher and Madge had told me to keep schtum for now, so schtum I was keeping. Albeit reluctantly.

Jan had no inkling of what we were keeping from her and I doubted whatever it was that had upset her this evening was anything to do with what we weren't telling her. It's complicated, but nothing to do with our relationship. Yesterday, a parcel had arrived at the police station, addressed to me.

An old shoebox, wrapped in a black plastic bag. I'd opened it, (yes, mindful, given the recent IRA bombing in London, that this could be a very dodgy package – but it was light in weight and didn't tick). It had smelled a bit whiffy, which should have been adequate warning. It's making me feel nauseous even thinking about it. I won't repeat what I'd said as I opened the shoebox lid. I'd turned quickly away and brought up my entire lunch into the DCI's metal wastepaper bin. I think it was only his extra experience that prevented him from doing the same, though he did go pretty green around the gills and had immediately opened the sash window. Inside was a dead animal. A ferret. The creature had been horribly mutilated. The note with it, formed of the clichéd cutouts from a newspaper (*The Sun*), simply read, *your next*. (Yes, 'your' not 'you're'.)

When we'd regained our stomachs, had a nip of the brandy that the DCI kept in his desk drawer, and the package had been collected for proper forensic analysis, the chief inspector filled me in about his suspicion, which was now more or less confirmed. So yesterday had gone something like this...

"Back in 1958," he told me, "my brother, Detective Inspector Richard Christopher, was murdered on his own doorstep. Shot at close range. We never caught his killer."

I knew most of this as it was common knowledge. When one of your own is murdered you don't forget it, even if it was a historic cold case.

"Prior to the shooting he and his wife received some disturbing packages – not disturbing on their own, but in hindsight, well..." He took a moment before carrying on. "They'd received a packet of rice, a tin of treacle, some fake eagle feathers and a dead weasel. These last few days we've received the same things. And now you've had this sent to you."

I was puzzled. "I'm sorry, sir, but I don't see the significance of these items?"

He seemed visibly shaken, highly unusual for my boss. He took a larger sip of the brandy and poured another splash into my glass. "Behind it all was the matter of unpaid debts. Debts that couldn't be paid.

Gambling debts that my brother owed. I knew nothing about them until he was dead, had no idea that he owed so much. Still don't know all of it."

"How much was 'much'?"

"The debts to the bookies and the off-licences? Those I found out about? Just under six-hundred pounds."

I whistled, shocked at the huge amount. Then said, "But I still don't see a connection? What has it to do with me? Why send this disgusting thing today?"

"No? How about this then? *Half a pound of tuppeny rice, half a pound of treacle. That's the way the money goes: pop goes the weasel?*"

I frowned. Still none the wiser.

"It's a children's nursery rhyme."

"Yes," I nodded, "I know that, but…"

"The rhyme is thought to be about pawning items to pay off debts. The second verse is about drunkenness. It goes: *Up and down the City Road, in and out of the Eagle. That's the way the money goes…*"

"*Pop goes the weasel,*" I finished for him.

"Exactly so, Laurie. Rice with a dollop of treacle was a cheap, sustainable food for the Victorian poor of London. They had little of value to pawn, but coats were worth a bob or two. Pawn them on the Monday, get them back on Saturday for church on Sunday, then the whole circle started again."

I frowned. Was a little concerned that he'd called me Laurie. It was always Walker while at work. This, I realised, was serious.

He explained some more. "Coat. Cockney rhyming slang. *Weasel and stoat,* coat."

Ah, that made some sense. "And the Eagle?"

"A famous pub on London's City Road. Still there, I believe. Go in with a pocketful of money on Friday after being paid, come out blind drunk and totally skint. Something, I'm afraid, that my brother, all too often, practised – though usually at the Rose and Crown in Walthamstow, not the Eagle in London."

"So he was murdered because he didn't pay off his debts?"

"That's what we thought at the time, but no, there was more to it than that. Bribery and corruption."

I chewed my lip, my mind working overtime. Was he implying what I thought he was implying?

He wiped his hand over his frowning face. "Nothing was ever confirmed, but I'm certain that my brother was bent. He was paying off his debts by turning a blind eye, losing evidence and falsifying statements."

DCI Christopher gulped down the rest of his brandy. "I suspect that he got himself killed by not doing something he was supposed to do."

"Or doing something he was *not* supposed to do?"

"Precisely."

"And these 'presents' have been turning up again?"

"They have. I didn't think much of a connection until this one this afternoon. Too coincidental. Too much the same M.O. Someone remembers the past and is set on resurrecting it."

"The same person repeating a same pattern? The same person, perhaps, who murdered your brother?"

The DCI puffed his cheeks. "Looks like it." He sat down in his chair, put the bottle of brandy away, I guessed because it was too tempting to have another glass.

"Yes, but," I remained puzzled. "I'm not a bent copper. I'm not in debt. Oh, apart from the 50p I owe the desk sergeant for that raffle he's organising for the Scouts."

"And I assure you, Laurie, I am not my brother. I don't gamble, I don't drink…" he laughed halfheartedly, pointed to our empty glasses. "Well, not often. And I am not corrupt. Never have been, never will be. Though there's been a few who've tried their luck to change my mind."

"Without success."

"Very much without success. My brother and I were different people, which probably added to the hostile difficulties between us. I was the bright, successful one who made a good marriage. He..." the DCI puffed his cheeks again, changed his mind and retrieved the brandy bottle, poured a small tot for us both. "My brother wasn't, didn't."

"His was not a happy marriage? Jan never says anything about her natural parents."

"Mainly because she doesn't remember much about them." He swallowed the brandy. "Jan's mum was a depressive nag, she was never right after losing Jan's twin sister. It was natural causes but Lettie always blamed herself. She didn't call a doctor in time, you see. She relied on sleeping pills for herself. My brother was on duty, though it was more likely that he was in the pub. By the time it was realised that the baby needed urgent attention it was too late. Then Richard was shot, leaving Lettie on her own and she couldn't cope. She hanged herself. Put a rope round her neck, tied one end to the landing banister rail and climbed over. Madge found her. We took Jan in, we'd been looking after her anyway, poor lamb."

"But you've done all right for her, sir. She's a super girl."

"Thank you, Sergeant. She is, and I intend to keep it that way. She knows little of this. Nothing at all about her father's reputation, or how her mother died."

It occurred to me that perhaps she should know, she wasn't a child now but as if reading my mind, the DCI answered my unspoken thought.

"We've not deliberately kept the truth from her, Laurie. At first, she was too young and then, well, she's never asked. If she does ask, then I, my wife… or now you, can tell her."

That was fair enough, and made sense. Some of the rest of it didn't.

"Why would someone be repeating something from the past? What motivation?"

The DCI pointed to where the wastepaper bucket had stood – now removed for a thorough washing out and disinfecting. He gave a small smile and went to the window to close it. "Revenge maybe? Except," he said, "this time it's a ferret not a weasel. Not many weasels around nowadays. They used to be pretty common in the fields alongside Sewardstone Road and on the edges of the Forest. Or whoever's responsible doesn't know the difference between a ferret, weasel or stoat."

I knew; I'd seen enough of all three in Devon where I'd lived since my younger days. "Ferrets are large creatures, stoats have a black tip to the tail but a weasel's tail is all brown. Weasels are weasily identified while stoats are stoatally different." Gallows humour, but it did raise a smile on the boss's face.

It soon faded when I said, "What about Joe Kass? He got pretty riled with you the other day, or so I heard."

"He blames me for his brother's suicide because I arrested him. A jury found him guilty of armed robbery, his prints were all over the shotgun used, and he was recognised by several reliable witnesses. He was guilty all right. If Joe had any connection to that crime there was never any evidence for it. So Kass might have a grudge against me, but as far as I know no reason to have had anything against my brother."

"Unless there was a debt to pay and your brother was supposed to have got Kass's brother off?"

The DCI shook his head. "Jan's father was killed in the April, Kass was caught and convicted much later in the year. So unless there's something I never found out about – like you say, a debt of some sort – this has nothing to do with Joe Kass. Besides, Kass had a cast iron alibi. When the shooting happened he was in hospital having a hernia seen to."

"So what do you suggest we do, sir?"

"Nothing much we can do. Why now after all this time? What's kicked the bucket over? And why target you today?"

I pondered a moment. "No clues from the past? Fingerprints, witnesses for these gifts being left?"

"Nothing from the past or present. And the only witness to the events of the past is Jan. She saw her father shot dead. It was fifteen years ago and she was five years old. She remembers nothing about it. And, for now, I intend to keep it that way." He looked at me sternly. I understood what he meant.

"Maybe check which prisoners have recently been released from jail?" I suggested. "Someone with a past grudge or who was owed money? Might explain the space between the years?"

"Could be. Worth checking. Will you make a start for me?"

"Of course, sir."

"Or it could be because Jan's father was shot on April 19th. Someone is sending a reminder, perhaps?"

That sounded sinister.

"But, Sergeant, not one word about today's unpleasant surprise to Jan – or my wife, come to that. Madge knows the connection between the rice, treacle and feathers, but not about this dead animal. I'd rather we kept it that way."

So, this uncomfortable Wednesday night I stood in the dark kitchen, mulling over yesterday afternoon's conversation. Did Jan, perhaps, know after all? Was she aware that there was something serious going on? More worryingly, had something – someone – frightened her this evening? She ought not to have come home alone. I ought to have been with her. This was all my fault! Should I go up to her? Apologise? Ask again what was wrong?

I thought back, recreating in my mind what I'd seen. Not much, to be truthful. We'd been working late, going through the sparse details of a case we were not getting very far with, finally calling it a day I'd pulled into the Ridgeway house forecourt from the direction of Mansfield Hill, from the south. We'd gone that way, not along the Ridgeway from the Station as the DCI had wanted to get some wine from the off-licence in Sewardstone Road before he closed up. The DCI had an account there and the manager, Tony Ashe, was a decent chap who sold good wine and spirits. I'd been watching from the front room window, waiting for Jan to get home. There were a few people about. I saw a couple crossing the road by Endlebury, but the nearest streetlight was on the blink so I didn't see them clearly. A couple, I thought, as he grabbed her hand and they ran for the bus which was pulling up at the stop, its hydraulic brakes hissing as they always did on a Routemaster. Jan had got off and crossed the road. Had I seen someone leaning out from the platform, waving to her? No, I think it must have been the couple getting on or the conductor.

I was being paranoid. Seeing, thinking, things that were not there. Should I leave? Should I write a note for her to find in the morning – or a note *not* apologising but explaining? Huh! Explaining what? That I had completely forgotten about booking a few days off? That I had completely forgotten about the circus and going out for a few days together? I'd even completely forgotten that it was Good Friday the day after tomorrow, idiot that I am.

Not an excuse, but a fact; the stress of trying to find the missing girl, Sally Armitage, had got to me. Not just me, the entire station. And now this other nasty business dredging up the past. What made it even worse between me and Jan was that this missing girl, strictly speaking, was not our case. DCI Christopher wasn't the lead investigating officer, that delight had fallen to Detective Chief Superintendent Brian Fellowes, a decent chap who did things by the book. Where kiddies were concerned, we all mucked in, all did what we could. Rank, who was in charge, who gave the orders was immaterial, the priority was to find the child alive and unharmed. If we could. Things were not too hopeful on that score.

I thought it disconcerting that Sally's father didn't seem particularly bothered that she was gone. Oh he cared, but 'stiff upper lip' only went so far. His insistent 'she'll come home when she's ready' somehow didn't strike true, nor did that attitude sit well with the distraught mother. We'd extensively interviewed them both, of course – by 'we' I mean Fellowes' team. A high percentage of assaults and killings were made through inter-family reasons so the father had been an initial suspect, but he had been at work in the Lesney's Matchbox factory over Hackney way until five that evening. Then he'd given a lift home to Wanstead to one of his co-workers, whose car had broken down. Spent over an hour tinkering together on the vehicle, and got home after seven to find police everywhere. A firm alibi, firmly corroborated. No way could he be responsible for Sally's disappearance.

I should say *step* father, for Sally wasn't Stanley Fairfax's child, nor was Sally's mother his wife; the pair were a couple but unmarried. Not that I'm saying anything about their marital status, that was their affair, not my place to judge although many others did. Even here in the seventies unmarried mothers are frowned upon, unmarried couples regarded as sinful. The relative freedom of the Swinging Sixties and the emergence of Women's Lib has done little to change the attitude of the older generation – of the younger as well, in some cases. It wasn't all Love and Peace.

Moral values are moral values I agree, but personally, I believe the relationship between a man and a woman, or a man and a man, come to that, of whatever religious belief, colour or creed is of no business to anyone except themselves.

The couple had three other children, three boys of eight, six and four. These were Fairfax's children. So regardless of morals or standards, do you see what I mean? He had his own sons, but the daughter was not *his* offspring. Did he truly care for her, or did he think of her as a cuckoo in the nest? Especially given her disability – disadvantage? I didn't know what to call her lack of stature. Her mother had explained it, an abnormality inherited from the man who had fathered her – a man long gone, and with no idea that he had a daughter, for Ms Armitage had admitted that the 'accident' had been a one-off indiscretion. She'd refused to be precise with any names, claiming the father's identity was insignificant and anyway she only had his first name, Gideon. Were there lies being told here? Did Stanley Fairfax resent the girl? Questions without answers. I seemed to have a lot of those piling up.

Sally had run away once before when she was eight and had been gone for several hours, but was found in Ridgeway Park riding on the miniature train that was a famous, unique, feature. It had turned out that she'd heard that back in the 1950s Mr Walt Disney, as an enthusiast, had once unexpectedly visited the miniature railway and had driven the train around the park's track for some time, only pausing for the press to take photographs. Sally, it seemed, had got it into her head that he would visit again and wanted to meet him and Mickey Mouse. Poor kid had, according to the police file, been desperately disappointed. Naturally, the park had been thoroughly searched from top to bottom this time round.

I went out into the hall, gazed up the stairs. All was in darkness. Dare I go up, tap on Jan's door and risk waking the DCI and Madge?

I let myself out, ensured that the front door was locked and drove away. Knowing I'd not get a wink of sleep I opted to walk around the area where Sally had disappeared, to search, again, under shrubs and bushes, to shine my torch over walls, and behind bins. To peer into shadows, then to sit on one of the seats opposite the closed library and reflect on what an absolute idiot I was.

14

A THURSDAY THOUGHT

No one said anything at breakfast, but I'm sure Aunt Madge guessed that something was up. It wasn't difficult to miss, I had black panda rings under my eyes and I looked like death warmed up. Add to that, Uncle Toby was well noted for being observant, even when he was supposedly buried in *The Times*.

"I'm repainting the banisters in the hall today," Aunt Madge announced brightly. "They're a bit world weary, so I thought a lick of brilliant white might cheer them up. No putting coats on the finial or rail when you both come home."

I nodded, miserably. A knock at the front door.

"You'd better get that," Uncle Toby said to me from behind his paper. "It'll be DS Walker." He peered over the top of the paper. "Might be an idea to make up?"

How did he *know* these things?

Given that neither he, nor my aunt, moved from the table I had no choice, but anyway, I realised that I needed to speak to Laurie about something that had been on my mind keeping me fitfully awake all night. No, two things, although one I wasn't sure about. *Let sleeping dogs lie* kept nagging in my head.

I answered the door. We both spoke at once.

"I'm sorry, I was…"

"Look, I'm sorry, I'm a…"

We laughed. Laurie gathered me into his arms in an enormous hug and all was forgotten and forgiven.

"Me first," I said, when he finished kissing me – a far more pleasant kiss than the unasked for, unwanted one Adrian Blessit had sneaked. *That* incident I immediately decided to bury and forget about. The other thing that was bothering me was a different matter.

He nodded, "Go on then. What's up, puss?"

I took a breath. "This might sound terribly silly but I had a thought last night."

"Oh no!" Laurie teased. "My girl having thoughts? How will I cope?"

I batted at his ear, not easy for he was taller than me and I had to stretch up. "Be serious. I was, as you know, at the circus yesterday. Some of the performers had visited Sally's school a few days before she went missing…"

He interrupted. "You think one of them kidnapped her? Not likely, they'd have to know her, where she lived, what route she took after school…"

I stamped my foot. "Will you listen! Some of those school visit performers were dwarfs. Very agile, very entertaining dwarfs. Given that we know Sally has a knack of chasing fanciful daydreams – that incident about Walt Disney for instance – what if she decided to run away to join the circus? Maybe she even thought that one of the men could be her father?"

Laurie frowned, I could tell that he was thinking, mulling over what I'd said.

"If that's the case, why haven't any of the circus folk come forward? Told us that she's there, or sent her home with a flea in her ear?"

"Aren't circus folk a bit like Romany Gypsies? Reluctant to have any truck with the police? Maybe, just maybe, her real father *is* one of them and he doesn't like the thought of Stanley what's-his-name, Sally's stepfather being responsible for her? Maybe her mother isn't telling the truth, maybe he knows he has a daughter and has been waiting his opportunity to claim her. For himself and for the circus. Maybe Sally turned up and hasn't told him the truth?"

I was aware that I'd proposed a lot of 'maybes' which could be fanciful nonsense. But what if they weren't?

"I think you'd better tell all this to your uncle. And for what it's worth, sweetheart, you might be onto something. Though I only said *might*."

15

CLIMB EVERY MOUNTAIN

As expected, the Thursday before Good Friday was manic at the library, not helped in the slightest by the decorating disruption. Admittedly, the men had got on pretty quickly, the ceiling done, most of the window frames repainted and there were a lot of windows – I'll tell you about those later. The staff room and 'facilities' were to be the last areas for a makeover, and these were scheduled for the Wednesday next when none of us, apart from Bert, would be in the building. I'd been reminded by Pam that as I was on leave next Tuesday, to clear my staffroom locker as the old ones were to be thrown out and replaced by new. We all rather hoped that these would be larger and more spacious for the benefit of storing our stashes of 'next to be read' books.

This Thursday, however, it was the turn of the entrance lobby to be painted. The interior entrance was a wood and glass-encased square space just inside the main double doors, and only needed a good clean down, but to either side were narrow corridor-type areas for the *In* and *Out* access. Both sides had large cork noticeboards on the walls, and small windows above a narrow bench-like seat at the end.

The main doors themselves were quite impressive from the outside, being almost castle-like in appearance. I don't know the architectural terms, but the wooden doors (oak?) were set beneath a semi-circular window, which in turn was beneath a Norman-style arched doorway.

The main doors were propped open in order to give the men a little more room to manoeuvre, and to keep the paint smell to a minimum, but there were ladders, pots of paint and dust sheets, so of course the entrance could not be used. A set of ladders was placed horizontally across the doorway, with a huge cardboard notice propped against them:

NO ENTRY - WET PAINT!
PLEASE USE THE STAFF DOOR
AT THE SIDE OF THE LIBRARY

It is beyond belief that people visiting a library could apparently not read.

If it wasn't so eye-rollingly baffling it would have been quite funny – at least ten people ignored the sign and clambered over the barricade of ladders, then stepped over the paint pots and inched their way round the overall-clad, brush-wielding decorators. The ladies holding their skirts close to stockinged legs, the gentlemen tutting.

What is the matter with people? Are they bonkers or something?

I did have to hide a laugh at one point as I watched a straight-faced Henry assist an elderly lady with her full of library books, pull-along shopping trolley to scramble over the ladders and then negotiate her way around the paint pots. She was so grateful, kept on thanking him for his gentlemanly courtesy. Joe, meanwhile, was quietly whistling something that vaguely resembled *Climb Every Mountain* from the *Sound of Music*.

Laurie, when he called in at about 11.30 had the sense to read the notice and come in the back way. He was smiling broadly as he approached the counter and I ceased flicking through the tray of tickets that I was attending to, and quickly crossed my fingers. Good news? Please be good news!

"We've found her!" Laurie announced loudly, so the person I was serving, and several who were nearby, turned their heads to listen.

"You were right," Laurie declared as he came round the counter to the staff side, grabbed hold of me and elated, twirled me round.

"Sally was with the circus people. Safe, well, unrepentant and cross that she has to go home, but that's for Welfare to sort, not us!"

Sy was sitting at his sound recordings desk rewinding cassettes. It was very annoying that people didn't return them with the tape wound back to the beginning, especially as there was no electric socket behind the desk to plug a tape machine into for this purpose. Sy had found that it was much quicker and economical to rewind the tapes by hand using a pencil inserted into the central hole ratchet. "What's the point of wasting power in a player," he'd say. "You want to keep the battery life for when you're rooster rocking." (He often spoke like this, in some form of alien language. We had no idea, half the time, what he meant.)

He heard Laurie's announcement and raising his voice broadcast the news to the entire library.

"Ladies and Gents! Your attention please! We have been informed by a representative of Chingford Constabulary that the missing girl, Sally Armitage, has been found safe and well!"

There came a moment's pause then a huge round of delighted applause and enthusiastic cheering from the public and the staff. And the decorators who perhaps should not have joined in as paint was spattering everywhere from Joe and Day-O's brushes.

Laurie explained a little further with as much as he knew. The circus people were too busy – or couldn't be bothered – to take notice of radio news bulletins or read local newspapers, and Sally hadn't been truthful about her age, claiming to be fifteen.

"Which, believe me," Laurie said, "can be easy to fake with good clothes, high heels, makeup and a padded bra! Add to that, her teachers all agreed that she has the talent of a very good, promising, actress."

He went on to add that Sally had taken her mother's compact, mascara, eyeshadow and lipstick; packed a few best clothes in a pillowcase and hidden everything inside her schoolbag, which she'd abandoned in the alley, after changing out of her school uniform. Dressed as an adult, she had not been noticed getting on the bus and once at the Big Top she'd spun a plausible cock and bull story about travelling from the south coast to join the circus troupe and no one had found reason to question her authenticity.

"Apparently, there's always young romantics wanting to join the circus," Laurie explained. "The owner – he's also the ringmaster – told me that these young hopefuls rarely last more than ten days, they soon get fed up with the hard work and disappear back home. They think the circus is all glitter and glamour, not realising that everyone has to pull their weight from dawn to midnight with all the background jobs from mucking out elephants to erecting the Big Top itself."

"It's hard enough putting up an ordinary canvas tent!" Sy interrupted. "I tried it once, never again!"

I didn't mention that I loved camping, as I wasn't sure what Laurie felt about holidaying in a tent. I'd have to ask him one day.

"None of you noticed her," Laurie added with a wry smile. "After a couple of rehearsals, she was competent enough as a performer to join the troupe with their old woman in a shoe routine."

"You mean she was there, in front of us?" I gasped.

Laurie nodded. "She was. Cheeky little monkey even said that she saw you ladies in the audience and waved."

I remembered! My goodness, cheeky monkey indeed!

Sy asked, "Will anyone be in trouble? Charged with kidnapping or anything?"

"No, it wasn't kidnapping. Sally wasn't being held against her will. All she had to do was walk to the bus stop and go home. No crime has been committed, although we did advise that the circus keep more of an ear to local news in future."

"Or you coppers could have used what limited brain cell capacity you have, and checked the circus out days ago." Joe's sarcastic comment was clearly heard.

"Leave it, Joe," Day-O responded as he tipped more paint into his paint tray. "The police do their best."

"Aye, their best to accuse the wrong people."

Laurie heard the exchange but ignored it. Instead, he thought it best to leave, his mission completed. "I'll see you later, sweetheart?"

I smiled, nodded. Would have liked to kiss him goodbye, but a queue was forming so I couldn't nip out the back with him. I blew him a kiss instead.

As the day progressed, word quickly spread with nearly everyone who came into the library (via the correct back door, or climbing over the ineffective ladder barricade), enquiring if the news was true. We were busy, but there were times, like this, when the world and his wife could have come in and we wouldn't have minded one bit about repeatedly answering the same question.

Good news was good news, after all.

16

WINDOWS AND
WHEELBARROWS?

Closing time that Thursday evening was a different matter. No one, except the staff, seemed to want to go home. The decorators had continued an hour into overtime in order to get finished, and the lobby, and the entire library, once they'd finally packed all their paraphernalia away, did look rather splendid although the paint smell had initiated a headache that continuously throbbed behind my temples.

Adrian had been a pain all day as well. By early afternoon I had come to the firm conclusion that I didn't like him. He'd followed me at lunchtime to the shops – I had a couple of things I had to get from Woolworths – pestering me to go to the cinema with him. He wouldn't take no for an answer, nor my insistence that I was engaged to Laurie and wasn't interested in anyone else.

"I'm not asking you to marry me!" he stated snidely, "just come to the flicks."

Yes, and sit in the back row where he'd have no intention of watching any of the film! I thought.

To shake him off, I nipped down the steps into the ladies' public lavatory on the Albert Crescent Island,

and waited there ten minutes. To my relief, when I re-emerged, he'd gone. Shame he wasn't gone for good, but that hope was rather like trying to catch lively rabbits with a lazy ferret.

I rediscovered him later that afternoon, to my enormous embarrassment, tucked around the corner near the wash basin in the library's ladies' loo. Assuming no one else was around, he and Trish were clinched together in a passionate embrace. They broke apart as soon as I opened the door, me bright red and backing out as quickly as I could, while Trish wriggled her dress and bra back to where they should be. Didn't she mind that he was older than her? I guessed not. They would both be for it if Pam or Henry Jones discovered what they'd been up to, but I wasn't a snitch. All I said to Trish, at my first opportunity of privacy, was that I had no intention of saying anything to anybody as long as it didn't happen again.

"What you do, with who, and where, is your business," I'd whispered (admitted somewhat primly), "but I suggest the ladies lav, or anywhere at work, is *not* the place." I desperately wanted to add that Adrian Blessit was not the person to do it with either, but if she wanted to make a fool of herself and get terribly hurt, that was her concern not mine.

For the rest of the afternoon and evening we didn't speak, staying away from each other as much as possible, even down to avoiding eye contact. For myself, I was annoyed with Trish for being so stupid, and him for being so blatantly fickle. He'd quickly moved from me to her. Mind you, Trish *had* been making doe eyes at him ever since he'd first walked into the library, so I wondered if this hadn't been their first liaison, simply the only time they'd been caught. Trish must have been cross when Adrian had jumped off the bus yesterday; did she know he'd then walked home with me and kissed me? Did she know he'd asked me to the cinema? Did she have *any* inkling that he was a deceitful toad who was only after sex and nothing else? I doubted it.

On the other hand, now that I knew about him and Trish I hoped that he'd leave me alone and it confirmed that I'd made the right decision about him. If Trish wanted him that was her look out. I had my Laurie, and Laurie was tons better than Adrian Blessit.

I don't think the rest of the staff noticed that Trish and I were keeping our distance. Nor that Adrian, probably for the first time in his entire life, actually concentrated on his work rather than arrogantly chatted someone up.

I breathed a sigh of relief when the final brush, dust sheet, ladder and whatnot were placed in the workmen's van and they drove off. They'd be back Tuesday, but I wouldn't, and by the time my leave was over, next Thursday, they'd be gone. For good, I hoped. What Trish thought I didn't want to know, or care. The sad thing, it looked like our friendship was well and truly over.

At ten minutes to eight, with closing time rapidly approaching, people were still coming in; that last minute – literally – rush to get books for the Easter break. It was nights like these that caused me the occasional nightmare. I would dream that I was on my own, shouting that we were closed. I'd shut and bolted the doors, but dozens of people were getting ladders from somewhere and were climbing in through the windows. And there was nothing I could do to stop them! Silly really, as no one could possibly climb in that way, as only the top half of the high windows opened. (There was a fixed handle on a ratchet to wind them open and closed.)

In my dream I shouted again and again, but people

continued to pour in, returning books by the wheelbarrow load. Yes! Really! No idea how they got the wheelbarrows through the windows, but that's the absurdity of nonsensical dreams. The books began to pile up into great mountains taller than myself. With one hand I was grabbing returned books, with the other stamping them out. In between, I was shoving books onto shelves. All the while desperately shouting, *We're closed! We're closed*! I'd woken Aunt Madge up at home several times with my dream-state incoherent moans. I knew I'd probably have another such nightmare tonight – if I managed to get to sleep, that is. I was exhausted, but guessed I'd be far too stressed to sleep.

But at last everyone *was* gone. The money for the fines float was counted and locked away in the safe, the lights were turned out, and with cries of "Goodnight!" and, "Happy Easter," (although Trish didn't say goodnight to me), we set off for home and a long, much looked forward to, weekend break.

I had forgiven Laurie, realising that he wasn't particularly interested in visiting Thoroughbred foals at a Newmarket racing yard, whereas Aunt Madge would love the opportunity to go with me. Poor Laurie, he was about as exhausted as I was. These last few days had taken their toll on him, and I did feel rotten about not understanding. I had no excuse, apart from selfishness. After all, I knew perfectly well what life with a policeman was like. Dad had been a policeman, although I hardly remembered those years, I was only five when he died. And I'd lived with Uncle Toby and Aunt Madge since then. I suppose things might have been easier if my uncle and Laurie were not so conscientious. Some of the believed corrupt coppers we knew of never seemed to be bothered by taking time off, or had wives disappointed by cancelled holidays. But then, they did not put the job or the enormous responsibility of it first and foremost, did they? I'd rather have Laurie morally honest and trustworthy at his job than the opposite.

As usual, Sy offered me a lift home, even though he was intending to set off to Margate for an Easter weekend of planned gigs at a well-known club venue. Not risking being broken into, he had brought his luggage – two suitcases and two guitars – into the library staff room for safe keeping. I helped him carry them to the car, and suggested a better way to pack everything into the boot. He had, I noticed, cleared out all the discarded rubbish.

He was terribly excited about his adventure, but had reined in his enthusiasm throughout the day, not wanting to bore us all. Once in the car, however, the previously closed floodgates opened.

"We've been rehearsing all week, got ourselves sorted with what we're going to play and in what order. This could be our big break, Jan. The place is rumoured to encourage managers' agents to sit in the audience looking for the next big name. It might be us, you never know!"

I didn't like to disillusion him that this was only Margate, not some superior London venue or the famous Cavern Club in Liverpool with people like Brian Epstein discovering The Beatles, Cilla Black or Gerry and the Pacemakers.

He enthused about the weekend ahead for the entire journey, even singing me a couple of verses from their planned repertoire. Despite his claim that he sounded like a donkey with a sore throat, I thought he had a fabulous voice. And actually, I thought he and his group deserved to be discovered.

"Just think," he grinned as he changed gear to

tackle the steep hill of Chingford Mount, "you might be sitting here with the next number one rock star!"

"If I am," I laughed, "I'll expect free tickets to your first sell-out Wembley concert, and I suppose you'll give up your day job?"

"Too right I will! The library's all right for now, but it hardly has the exciting atmosphere of the Isle of Wight Festival, or the new Pyramid Stage at Glastonbury, does it?" He grinned to himself, delighting in his daydream fantasy. "Think on it Jan, to play where T Rex, Bowie, Joan Baez and Fairport Convention have all stood."

I quite liked Bowie and Joan Baez, but wasn't a great Mark Bolan fan. And was he really hoping to become a headliner at the increasingly popular Glastonbury Festival in Somerset? Especially if he wasn't keen on camping. The festival was notorious for becoming a mud bath. I had a friend who'd been to the festival saying that she didn't worry about getting her clothes caked in mud because she simply took them all off. I didn't want to burst his bubble so let him prattle on. No one likes their parade rained on, do they?

Sy parked outside our house, still enthusing about a possible famous future. I wasn't totally listening, just making pretend interested noises every so often. I watched a bus pull up ahead of us at the bus stop. Two people, a couple, got off and walked away arm-in-arm. I expected the man who had been waiting on the pavement to board it, but he remained leaning against the concrete bus stop post. Perhaps he was waiting for someone? The bell rang and the bus pulled away, trundled off towards the terminus in Station Road.

It was growing dark, and the house gates were open. Laurie was parking Uncle Toby's car. He must have seen us because he waved. I waved back.

"Look," I suggested to Sy, "Aunt Madge always

cooks too much, and I think it's her delicious chicken casserole tonight. There'll be plenty to go round if you want to join us. You've a long drive. Have some dinner first?"

He was hesitant, unsure, but I pressed him and seeing the sense of my suggestion, gave in. "You sure your aunt won't mind?"

"She'll mind if you *don't* come in!" I laughed. "Pull onto our frontage, the car will be quite safe there."

"OK. Thanks." Sy started the engine again and reversed slightly so that he could swing easily in through the gates without scraping any of his paintwork on the brick pillars. He parked next to Laurie's green Morris Minor and switched the engine off. I got out, (as inelegantly as always), and went to give my fiancé a firm hug and a warm hello kiss.

As Sy got out from his driver's side, his hand outstretched towards Laurie, I heard three loud bangs in quick succession.

17

INTERLUDE: DS LAURIE WALKER

I watched Simon Henbury-Clive pull up outside the house. I knew Jan liked him, although I thought he was a know-it-all, possibly unjustly, as I had in my mind an amalgamation of misplaced jealousy and a rection against his snobby, Eton-type upper class, plummy voice. Which was ridiculous of me because he wasn't posh or a snob, and I had no idea whether he'd been to Eton or not. In all probability, not. It was merely that he'd rubbed me up the wrong way from the first time I'd met him towards the end of January when he'd started work at the library.

I don't know how or why my hostility had originally manifested itself, but we were like a pair of growling dogs with hackles raised snarling over a mouldy old bone. Which rather makes it sound like I'm referring to Jan as the old bone doesn't it? Again, totally ridiculous as Jan had no interest, romantically, in Sy and as far as I could tell he wasn't interested in her beyond being agreeable colleagues. So I think my silly jealousy might have been because of his musical ability. And there I did have to admit some envy.

He was very talented. The riffs he played on that

guitar of his were out of this world. I'd never been able to master a guitar, although I was a pretty decent piano player. Was it, maybe, that I secretly would have liked to have been in a band? Maybe in my late teens I'd thought about it as most teenage boys do, but to pursue it as a serious ambition? No. Facing facts, I didn't have the talent, inclination or necessary dedication that Sy obviously had. To play tunes on the piano at family Christmas and birthday gatherings was enough for me. The money these big rock stars earned was alluring, but how many small, pub-gig level, bands manage to reach the dizzy heights of top ten fame? Not many. Besides, I was a policeman and, on the whole, I loved my job. Most of the time.

I'd parked the DCI's Jag in the garage and locked the garage door, then waited by my own car for Jan to get out of that totally impractical vehicle of Sy's. My small personal relief, she didn't much care for it.

"What's the point of a car that doesn't have room for a couple of saddles and a few bags of horse feed?" she often said.

I frowned when he reversed slightly then turned in through the gates, realising that Jan must have asked him in. That's all I wanted after a long day at work, having to pretend to like the chap and make an effort to be polite to him. Hopefully, he only needed to nip to the loo or something, but it was odds-on that Jan had invited him to stay for dinner as a thank you for bringing her home. Which, OK, was fair enough and I was grateful that he put himself out to give her a lift home on her late nights. I didn't like her being out on her own. Eight o'clock wasn't late and there were usually plenty of people around, but she'd come home on her own yesterday, after that jaunt to the circus. I guess that's the downside of being Police, I know the dangers of the outside world, the muggings, the assaults, the rapes. Aye, and worse. Of course I wanted Jan to be safe. Something had bothered her last night, I'd picked that much up. Maybe she'd tell me about it in her own good time, I wasn't going to press her – another downside to being a policeman, an innocent question could all too easily turn into the Spanish Inquisition.

Was it because of some sort of insecurity or self-doubt that I harboured these irrational feelings against Sy? This ongoing conviction that his band was going to soon be the best thing since sliced bread irritated me, but if he wanted to dream that was his lookout, as long as the disillusion didn't pounce too hard at some point. His repeated assurance that all they needed was for someone in the know to sign them up for a recording contract was wearing thin. His band was good, he was brilliant, but to match the likes of the Stones, Genesis, Wings or Pink Floyd? Not a hope. But I guess we all need our dreams to get us through the dreariness of everyday life. I simply wished that he kept his dreams to himself.

Another irritation, this evening I wanted to celebrate finding the missing girl, Sally, with Jan and her family. The DCI had stopped off at his off-licence especially to buy a bottle of champagne for this purpose. We didn't usually go overboard when we successfully completed a case, but this time the result had been a good one, and anyway the DCI had explained that it was a sort of anniversary for him and his wife. Despite the tragedy that had occurred on the same date those years later, they liked to remember a happier event. During the war, Sunday April 19th had been the occasion of their first official date.

"I saw her at the evening church service sitting by herself a few pews in front of me," my guvnor had said as we'd left the Station. "As we filed out, I plucked up courage to ask if I could walk her home." He'd laughed at the memory. "I'd not realised that her home was five miles away, or that she cycled to and from work at Bletchley Park. She left the bike and walked with me. That was no problem, but I then had to walk back again, by which time it was late and all the doors were locked. I had to climb up the wisteria to get into a first-floor window."

I somehow couldn't imagine DCI Christopher shinning up a wisteria vine and crawling in through a window. Although he'd been several years younger back then.

Madge, Mrs Christopher, was a lady through and through – literally. Her father, Major Sir Douglas Bolton-Chalmers had been killed in action at Dunkirk, her mother was Lady Julia Bolton-Chalmers, the third daughter of the Earl of Hembledon. So if anyone should have airs and graces you'd have thought it to be Madge, but apart from the fact that she spoke well, (in several languages), and knew all about etiquette, you'd never have guessed her status. She was ordinary and down to earth, although she didn't take any nonsense from anyone, and had little patience with outright fools.

Was I being an outright fool this evening? I suspected that Madge would say I was. And Jan.

So I swallowed any irrational feelings of being annoyed as Jan got out of the car and called that Sy was going to join us for dinner. I had a lot to make up with Jan, as I'd been an ass through and through these last few days, and although I wanted to tell her, privately, that I'd managed to wangle a few days off over Easter after all, I mentally pledged to turn a leaf over and stop being stupid. Sy was coming to dinner, not moving in permanently. I had the rest of the evening to offer to take Jan somewhere special tomorrow or Saturday.

Somewhere of her choosing. I fixed a smile to my face as she came up to me to give me what was probably a most undeserving – but extremely welcome – kiss. I couldn't help but think how beautiful she was, and how very, *very* much I loved her.

Then I heard a bang and something sharp hit me in the side, slamming against my ribs. It felt as though someone had hit me with a rounders bat or metal bar. I thought, *Sod it, that's going to leave one bugger of a bruise.*

I heard two more bangs in quick succession and my thigh felt as if I'd been punched or kicked by one of Jan's horses. Jan was screaming. I think I heard Madge's voice shouting something, then telling me to be still, but I wasn't sure why I was lying down on the hard ground. It was getting difficult to breathe, my leg was on fire, and I wondered who'd dimmed the forecourt lights because everything was becoming darker than it had been.

Did I hear sirens? I don't know; I might have imagined them.

18

THE SMELL OF PAINT

Aunt Madge and Uncle Toby appeared almost immediately after those three loud bangs. My aunt bent over Sy who was slumped against the front wing of his car, his chin on his chest.

"Jan? Are you all right?" she called to me. I was standing there, my hands on my cheeks, like a stone statue, frozen with fear.

"Jan?" she repeated. I nodded. I couldn't speak.

She ran to Laurie. He was on the ground with a lot of blood on his shirt, and his trousers. Pooling beneath him. My aunt undid his tie and bound it tight round the top of his leg, then yanked off her cream silk blouse, several buttons popping off, and bunched it into a ball which she clamped over his left side. Uncle Toby had sprinted past us to the open gates. I watched, terrified, as he dashed across the road, causing cars to screech to a halt. He hurtled on down Endlebury Road. It was dark, but the street lights showed someone running ahead of him. Whoever it was, turned into the concealing hedges of the park entrance. I stood where I was beside Sy's car, unable to move or think beyond the thought that it was silly to head for the park because the gates would be closed and locked. I could feel more screams churning tight in my chest. Aunt Madge turned towards me, not moving her hand from where it was pressing down on her bloodied blouse.

"Jan. Jan dear, listen to me. Keep calm but run indoors, call an ambulance and the police, then *stay* there indoors."

I heard her voice as if it came from a great distance away. I was rooted to the spot.

"Jan!" she yelled. "*Move! Now!*"

That broke the spell, I raced inside, reeled as the lingering smell of fresh paint hit my senses, wondered, stupidly and rather incongruously, if the library decorators were here, then I vaguely remembered that my aunt had said she was going to repaint the stair banisters, which explained the smell. It wouldn't have taken her long to do, a couple of hours this morning, and everything was now back where it belonged, except there was usually a coat or two left temporarily on the acorn-shaped finial of the bottom newel post. Coats, and my uncle's Fedora hat that he always wore when out and about, were now neatly hung on the coat hooks on the wall. Aunt Madge was always complaining that coats belonged on their hooks, not on the bannisters.

I grabbed the telephone receiver and fumbled at the dial. My hands were shaking, and I clumsily knocked over the vase of fresh daffodils that my aunt had put on the telephone table yesterday. The vase crashed to the wooden floor and smashed into pieces, water and yellow flowers spilling over the rug. I dialled 999, asked for ambulance and police. Answering the lady at the other end on autopilot I managed to give precise information of the address and the circumstances, saying that my boyfriend was a policeman. I wasn't sure whether the last bit was to the emergency operator or to myself as I replaced the receiver and plonked myself, with an unsteady thump onto the bottom stair, the numbness returning inside and out, aside from the uncontrollable shaking that was engulfing me.

Laurie and Sy had been shot. That much my seized-up brain had taken in, but at that moment it was something else I was picturing in my mind. I could suddenly, and out of the blue, remember every small detail of the night when my dad had been murdered. Everything had come back to me as if it had happened yesterday, not fifteen years ago to the very day.

I don't know how long I sat there in a sort of trance, it seemed like hours, but Uncle Toby roused me to awareness by putting his arms round me and holding me safe and tight. It had only been about fifteen minutes, I think. I buried my face in his shoulder and started to sob. His hand stroked my hair, and gradually I heard what he was gently saying.

"*Shh*, Cupcake, an ambulance will be here soon. Detective Chief Superintendent Brian Fellowes has just arrived with DS Pete Mulliner and Sergeant Tanner. Others are on their way."

Cupcake, my uncle's affectionate nickname for me. I looked up at him, stammered, "Laurie?"

"Madge knows what she's doing."

"I need to be with him," I whispered, trying, unsteadily, to get to my feet.

"Of course, but all in good time. Ah, there's the ambulance, let the medics do their job first, eh?" The siren wailed louder and the reflection of blue lights flashed through the open front door into the house.

It didn't occur to me, at that point, that my uncle was deliberately keeping me away from outside. I blew my nose on the man-sized cotton handkerchief he handed me. Another man had come into the hall, a tall chap, grey haired, serious faced. I recognised him as DCS Fellowes.

"All secure," he said to my uncle in a low, gruff, voice. "You didn't manage to catch the bugger then? I don't suppose you got a look at him?"

"No. Lean, agile, about my height. Denim jeans, leather jacket. Dark hair. Could have been anyone. He shinned over the gate into the park with no problem. Already had too much of a start on me. Not a good idea for me to go alone into the park after him."

"I should think not! He's armed. You shouldn't have even given chase. Nor let your wife go out there until all was secure. Might have been more than one of them."

My uncle said, blandly, "In the circumstances, would you have stayed put? A policeman down and my niece out there, vulnerable?"

I was miles away so his words didn't properly register, although somewhere at the back of my mind a voice was whispering that if someone was shooting a gun you stayed where it was safe and secure, and did not run direct into a possible line of fire.

The superintendent chuckled. "Probably not." He glanced around, bent to pick up the scattered, battered, daffodils and put them down in a ragged heap on the telephone table. "The team will get the park sealed off and the dogs will be there soon. The bastard won't get far. We'll get him."

I heard all these words but didn't take any of them in, not much of it made sense to my muddled mind. The screams were still there, tight in my chest. I wanted to clamp my hands over my ears, to stop the words and to stop the roaring that I could hear inside my brain, but I couldn't move a single muscle.

Uncle Toby put one finger under my chin and tipped my stricken face upward. "Cupcake? Do you feel up to talking to DCS Fellowes? He'll be in charge of this case. We need to know. Did you see anything? Anyone?"

I bit my lip as I gazed direct into my uncle's concerned, kind, eyes. "I was upstairs, in bed, telling a story to Bee Bear, my teddy. Daddy was in the hall painting the skirting board where it had been scuffed by my dollies' pram. The one you'd given me as a present. Mummy was cross about the scuffs, she said I'd scraped the paint deliberately. I hadn't. She made me put the pram in the shed. I didn't like to leave it out there because of the spiders."

Uncle Toby was frowning, but he let me continue speaking.

"The covers got damp and started to smell. I didn't like that smell, nor did my teddy. I don't think I had any dolls, did I? I wheeled Bee Bear round in the pram."

"You did, along with the cat," Uncle confirmed.

"I hated the smell of the stinky paint that Daddy was using, but I liked hearing his whistling. I got out of bed and went to sit on the stairs. He was whistling nursery rhymes. *Jack and Jill* and *Sing a Song of Sixpence*. Mummy didn't know I was there. She'd come out of the kitchen, she had soapsuds all over her hands from the washing up, I remember because she fiddled with the daffodils that were in a vase on the telephone table and left soapy bubbles over them. She was grumbling that Daddy should have put more newspaper down because the brush was dripping paint onto the carpet." I paused and scowled, remembering my mother. "Mummy was always grumbling about something, wasn't she?"

Uncle Toby sighed, a sound that conveyed a great sadness. "I'm afraid she was, and usually for no specific reason, but your mother was very depressed.

She never came to terms with the death of your twin sister."

A thought struck me, something that had never occurred to me before. "Was it my fault that June died?"

"Good heavens, no!" Uncle exclaimed. "Whatever made you think that? June succumbed to pneumonia, a residue of a particularly bad attack of whooping cough. You had whooping cough too, but not as bad. June's death was no one's fault unless you want to blame the frailties of a premature birth, and the ambivalence of nature."

I chewed my lip, had to accept what he had said, though I wasn't sure why I had always thought that the death of my sister had somehow been my fault. I'm sure that Mummy had blamed me. Perhaps I'd been the one to catch whooping cough first and had passed it on?

I returned my thoughts to that night when Daddy had been murdered. "Mummy went back into the kitchen and someone knocked at the front door. Daddy answered it, and he sounded cross. 'What the...?' he said, and then there was a loud bang."

Gradually, I noticed that Uncle Toby and DCS Fellowes' frowns had deepened. I stared at them, my scrutiny going from one man to the other, and finally realised that although they'd allowed me to talk, they were both looking very confused.

"I've remembered nearly everything from the night Daddy was killed," I explained. "It's all, suddenly, come back to me."

Uncle exchanged another glance with the Detective Chief Superintendent.

"This evening's events, the sounds and smells seem to have triggered a locked-away memory," DCS Fellowes suggested. "I've heard it happen before."

"*Mmm hmm,* looks like it," my uncle nodded.

I realised that I'd been talking about the *wrong* murder. I felt more sick than ever.

"Go on," Uncle Toby urged, "while you can recall it all."

I paused a moment. Why wasn't I talking about what had happened outside? About Sy and… and Laurie. And then I understood that I didn't *want* to talk about it, didn't want to talk about… about… If I didn't *think* about it, perhaps I could convince myself that nothing had happened?

I switched my mind back to when I was five years old.

"There was a loud bang and Daddy fell against the wall. There was blood all over the hall wallpaper, and Daddy had dropped the paintbrush onto the carpet. The man stood there, just inside the door, he was laughing. He had a black balaclava hat on so I could only see his eyes and mouth. There was a gap in his teeth, one at the front bottom was missing." I remembered wondering whether the tooth fairy had given him sixpence for it.

"Mummy came from the kitchen and the man fired his gun at her. He missed, but she knocked the telephone table and the vase of flowers over. I'd helped her pick them from the garden that morning. The telephone tinkled as it fell, it broke. Daddy tried to grab the post at the bottom of the banisters but the man fired his gun at him again. There was blood everywhere, all over Daddy, on the carpet, all over the big flower pattern of the wallpaper along the hall. Mummy was screaming and I screamed too."

I drifted into silence, fighting more rising screams that wanted to get out. "It's funny," I said, "up until now I didn't remember anything about sitting on the stairs, Daddy whistling, or Mummy grumbling. I've always thought that I was in bed and heard the bangs."

"You were five years old, sweetheart," Uncle Toby said, "no one expected you to remember everything as it really happened."

"Was this all real then?" I asked.

He nodded. "You were sitting on the stairs when I arrived, clutching Bee Bear, but you never said a word about any of it. Not until now."

"Can you remember anything else about this man?" The DCS asked, squatting down on his heels to be nearer my face level.

"He was skinny, not very old, I think. He had drainpipe trousers and winklepicker shoes, although I didn't know they were called that, then."

There was something else as well, something I knew I ought to remember, but it was illusive, I couldn't quite access it, although I knew that whatever it was it could be important. I shook my head to clear it of the throbbing that was building behind my eyes and glanced at my hands. I thought how pretty my engagement ring looked, sparkling beneath the overhead hall light. The diamond caught the flashing blue light of the ambulance, bringing me right back to the present.

Aunt Madge came into the hall. Her face was white and drawn, she wore a skirt and fluffy slippers, and on the top half a man's jacket rested on her shoulders to cover her bra and lacy silk slip. The silk was covered in blood, as were her skirt and hands in which she carried something frilly. I realised it was her best cream blouse, now ruined and soaked in blood from where she'd used it as first-aid padding. DCS Fellowes only wore a shirt and waistcoat, no jacket. He must have placed his around Aunt Madge for warmth and her modesty when he'd arrived.

She slipped the jacket off and handed it to him. "Thank you for the loan, Detective Chief Superintendent. I've done all I can outside, and the medics have taken over. The ambulance will soon be ready to leave," she said, sounding exhausted. "Will you go with Jan, Toby, while I clean up and change? I'll follow with the car."

Uncle took my hands in his and his touch felt warm; my hands were cold, ice cold. "We'll get all you've told us about your dad written down and sorted as soon as we can, Cupcake, but do you recall anything about tonight? What happened? We need to know darling, it's urgent."

Aunt Madge's appearance brought this night's evil happening to the forefront of my mind. I wanted to shout and scream and tell them all to go away – I wanted to run away, hide in some dark, quiet place where I could think and sort things out. But knew I couldn't do any of that.

In almost a whisper, reluctant, I explained that Sy had pulled up in the main road and I'd asked him in to join us for dinner. We'd got out of the car, and… "I didn't see anyone."

I looked at Uncle Toby and then at Aunt Madge. I said, "The people who got off the bus, or the man standing at the bus stop, might have seen someone, though?"

"What man was this?" DCS Fellowes almost barked, getting to his feet and managing to control his frustrated urgency.

"I thought I'd already said?" I murmured. I'm sure I had. Obviously not. "There was a man waiting at the bus stop. But," I hesitated, swallowed, gathered my disorientated, muddled, thoughts. "But he didn't get on the bus when it stopped. He ignored it."

I swallowed down nausea, and realised something

else. "He didn't even look at the bus, he was watching me and Sy in the car."

"Did you see his face?" DCS Fellowes asked slowly, not fiercely, but I could hear the desperate need for an answer in his tone.

I stared at him for a moment, blinked back threatening tears a few times. Then nodded.

"I couldn't see him clearly when he was at the bus stop because his face was in shadow, but when he came towards our gate I recognised him straight away. It was Adrian Blessit."

19

ANY NEWS?

Uncle Toby held my hand all the way to the hospital in the ambulance, and barely let go, even when we got there and sat for what seemed a lifetime in a bleak, uncomfortable corridor. I think he was as frightened as I was. Certainly as anxious. He kept rubbing my knuckles with his thumb; his touch, his presence, was so needed. I don't know what I would have done without him, nor Aunt Madge when she eventually joined us.

"Any news?" she whispered as she sat down next to me so that I was sandwiched between her and Uncle Toby.

I shook my head, I didn't really comprehend what was going on. Every time a doctor or nurse appeared we'd look up, hopeful, fearful, wanting news but not wanting news.

After a while – I've no idea how long – Uncle Toby disappeared to make a telephone call. He looked grim as he rejoined us, handed Aunt Madge and me a cup of what was meant to be coffee.

"I've spoken to DCS Fellowes. They secured the park pretty quickly, sent the dogs in." He puffed his cheeks, stroked my hand again. "They got him. Blessit is in custody. They'll want statements from you, of course, but the dogs also found the gun. Had his fingerprints all over it. He's claiming he's innocent, naturally, they always do, but he hasn't got a leg to stand on."

A white-coated doctor appeared, and at last, didn't walk past but stopped to talk to us.

"You'll be relieved to hear that the operation was a complete success. No serious internal injury, apart from a couple of broken ribs, substantial oedema and muscle trauma. We've removed the bullet and patched him up. The second bullet to the thigh went straight through, again no serious damage but he's lost a lot of blood, so recovery will take a while and he'll be sore for some weeks. There shouldn't be any lasting damage, but these things often take time to heal, mentally and physically. The bullet we did retrieve is already on its way to your forensic people, DCI Christopher. They'll be wanting it for evidence, I assume?"

My Uncle nodded, grim. "Indeed. It'll need to be matched to the gun."

"Can... can I see him?" I asked tentatively, scared that the doctor might say no, equally as scared that he might say yes.

"He'll be out for a few hours yet, my dear. I suggest, go home, have something to eat, get some sleep and come back tomorrow..." he glanced at a clock on the wall. It had a monotonous clicking tick which was so irritating that at one point I'd been tempted to knock the thing off the wall and smash it.

"I mean later this morning, it's already well into tomorrow. I'm sure the young man would far rather wake up to see your pretty face relaxed and smiling, rather than the, forgive me for being truthful, rather than the pale, drawn and blotched visage you're currently sporting."

They say the truth can hurt, but I couldn't begrudge the doctor because I'd seen what I looked like in the mirror in the ladies' loo. Pale, drawn and blotched was actually a kind understatement.

Uncle Toby drove home, Aunt Madge sat in the back with me, her arm around my shoulder, I think for mutual comfort.

There was no doubt; the ambulance men had said it, and the doctor and two nurses. My aunt, because of her quick thinking and knowledge of first aid had very probably saved Laurie's life.

There had been nothing she could do for Sy. Shot through the heart, he had been dead before he'd slumped to the ground.

20

INTERLUDE: DS LAURIE WALKER

Much of the following few weeks was a blur, some of it, at the beginning, because the hospital kept poking needles into me, which contained various sedatives and knocked me out. I'm not complaining. I hurt. A lot. Unconscious sleep was a welcome bliss.

Hospital beds and hospital wards are not comparable to comfortable five-star hotels, or even your own bed come to that. The hospital bed was a barely tolerable plank of wood but the staff were fabulous, especially the nurses, even the dragon of the ward, Sister Bridgit Mahoney. They certainly all looked after me. I like to think because I was a model patient, but I've a suspicion that it was because Madge had plied them with Easter eggs that she'd bought as shop leftovers.

I don't know how I would have got through those first uncomfortable days without Jan by my side – even if she did eat the chocolate eggs that were meant for me.

My mum and dad came up from Devon soon after the Easter holiday. Jan had instructed them not to make the journey until the Tuesday as the trains weren't running well over the holiday period, and anyway I was asleep for most of that time. Assuring them that I was out of danger, she persuaded them to see the sense of waiting. All the same, I was glad to see them that first afternoon when they walked into the ward, (with more Easter eggs). Both Mum and Dad were relieved to see for themselves that I was doing OK. For their sake, I tried to hide the wincing and suppress the groans whenever I had to move my leg.

After the first week my befuddled brain was starting to make sense of things again, although I continued to sleep a lot. Damage to my thigh was, very fortunately, not as severe as it could have been. The bullet had damaged the muscle but missed the bone and arteries, although the healing of muscle tissue, I assure you, is not to be sniffed at. Those first weeks, we had to be careful of infection and believe me, those physiotherapist sadists would do well as Russian James Bond torture advisors.

In films and on TV when the hero gets shot, he's usually up and about again within a few days. (Or in the case of Bond, cavorting in the lead female's bed.) A great pity that real life is *nothing* like the movies.

I'm not complaining; my rehabilitation meant I could spend a lot of time with Jan, and once I was sort of mobile again, (albeit with the aid of a walking stick and her arm), we went out for several jaunts, courtesy of dear Madge doing the driving – at least until Jan, bless her, learned to drive, took her test and passed it first time.

Under arrest and charged with murder and attempted murder, Blessit initially denied the accusation, but once it became clear that too much evidence was stacked against him, he changed his plea, admitted his guilt and was eventually locked up for a long time. I had no sympathy for him.

Not that imprisonment would make up for the discomfort I went through, or that he'd brutally killed Sy, a young man who'd had a potentially exciting life ahead of him.

One huge regret: I was unable to attend Sy's funeral, although Jan, Madge and the DCI went. It was at his home town in Buckinghamshire, a sad occasion made worse by the utter senselessness of his death. As Jan had told me, he'd been so looking forward to doing that gig in Margate, so hopeful of achieving his dream. And, rethinking my stupid prejudice against him, I realised that he probably would have done, too. He was a very good musician. Throughout my recovery I couldn't help but feel guilty that I'd initially thought ill of him. My mistake, one I'd never be able to amend.

I did, however, have the chance to speak privately to DCI Christopher one afternoon shortly before the hospital kicked me out. I told him about how guilty I felt. That maybe the wrong man had died, that it was my fault Sy had died. I received a rollicking for that.

"Look, son," the DCI had answered, somewhat gruffly, "*you* didn't fire that pistol, *you* didn't aim it at someone with the intention of shooting to kill. The only one to blame is Blessit himself. Not you."

"But I don't understand why he did it?" I countered. "What was his motive?"

The DCI didn't answer straight away, then opened up. "From what I can tell, there was no reason, except the bruising to his own ego. He fancied pretty young women, but Jan preferred you. And poor Sy, sadly, he resented him because he was well off financially. Blessit is to blame, Laurie. Not you. You didn't pull that trigger. He did."

It took a while for his words to sink in, but he was right.

21

AFTERMATH OF A MURDER

Those first few days when Laurie was in hospital were probably the worst days of my adult life. In between hospital visits, welcoming Laurie's mum and dad, and looking after them while they stayed with us, I'd had to give full statements at the police station.

There was no doubt that I had recognised Adrian Blessit while he'd lounged, waiting for us, at the bus stop. Did he realise that I'd seen him? Had one of those shots been meant for me? I assume that DCS Fellowes had probably asked him those questions, but if there were any answers given I never knew about them. Nor did I want to know.

My witness statement, Blessit being found hiding in the park, his fingerprints on the gun, the bullets matching that same gun... he pleaded guilty in the hope of a reduced sentence. I'd have been quite happy had hanging not been abolished in 1969.

But there was a second statement that I had to make, and this one was more difficult. I had been five years old when my father had been killed, and I knew that anything I said now would be treated with scepticism, at least until proof came to light. There was that one thing that had eluded me, though. I knew, somewhere in my mind, that if only I could concentrate I would be able to identify the man. It was there, the knowledge was there, but shut behind a locked door and I had no idea where my five-year-old self had hidden the key.

And then one afternoon, while visiting Laurie in hospital, the key appeared and the door was flung wide open.

I was making my way along the balcony-like walkways which linked the distinctive Edwardian towers of the Whipps Cross hospital building. The wind and rain were scuttling across the open parapets, so I was hurrying, head down and, not seeing the warning signs, nearly bumped straight into a man who was repainting the much-scuffed doors at the far end. I apologised profusely, but he only laughed.

"No harm done, miss." He had a friendly, proper belly laugh; head back, mouth open. He was elderly, a volunteer odd-job man I reckoned. His hair was grey and several of his teeth were missing.

I carefully edged through the open doors, minding the fresh paint – and stopped dead.

The old boy was whistling beneath his breath, not a tuneless whistle like Joe Kass had been wont to do, but... And the last piece of the puzzle dropped into place. I had missed something. Or rather, missed something that *had* been missing.

My dad lay dying, two fatal shots to his chest. Mum was standing in the hall, screaming. The front door was wide open and I sat on the stairs, clutching my teddy bear, watching the man who had killed my daddy walk away down the front garden path. He opened the gate, walked through, turned, shut the gate behind him. He wore grey, woolly gloves, so no finger prints, and a knitted, black balaclava which covered most of his face.

He had looked straight at me, laughed, then said something that had made no sense to me at that age. I remembered that he'd had a tooth missing, and recalled the exact words he'd spoken. The words slammed into my mind now as I stood beside those partially painted hospital doors. Older, I fully comprehended those words, and realised that the gap caused by a missing tooth would probably have received dental attention at some point during the interim fifteen years. The voice might have changed slightly, but *the gap would no longer be there*!

Poor Laurie, I briefly explained that I *had* to urgently speak to Uncle Toby, so I terminated my visit and hailed a taxi to take me straight to Chingford Police Station. My uncle listened to me, sceptical at first, but his enthusiasm grew. He picked up the telephone, barked down it that he wanted all the evidence relating to the murder of my father brought to his office – and wanted it yesterday.

Going through those old files together, it was evident that much of what I'd said to Uncle Toby that evening when Laurie and Sy had been shot, were echoed by my mother's statement and what the attending police had found.

The bullets that had killed my daddy were from the same gun that had killed Sy and nearly killed my Laurie. For the first time I found out about those strange things left for us to find, the treacle, the feathers and photographs of those dead animals. Also for the first time, I discovered that these recent 'gifts' were a copycat of the original ones. My dad had received almost the same things, years ago. I was cross that the facts had been kept from me; understandable when I was a child, but these latest things were a different matter. Would knowing have made any difference?

Would it have saved Sy's life? Probably not, but I did wonder.

Joe Kass, we now knew, owned the gun and had been charged for not holding a licence for it. Adrian Blessit admitted that he'd known his uncle had it hidden away, a relic from the war, and that he'd taken it with the deliberate intention of mowing Laurie down. Sy's death had been unintentional. He'd been aiming at me.

But there was more to uncover.

Under suspicion of murder, Joe Kass had been questioned again, and Uncle Toby relayed the outcome to Laurie, Aunt Madge and I as we sat round Laurie's hospital bed the next evening.

"Kass confessed that he'd been furious with my brother, Richard, because he owed a lot of money from unpaid gambling debts. Poker, apparently. They'd served in the same platoon where substantial I.O.Us had been promised by Richard, but they never materialised."

Uncle Toby said that he had never discovered who his brother had owed money to. Now we knew at least one of the names.

"He owed Joe Kass a lot. If he'd paid it, Kass could have bought the decorating business, not Henry Jones, and he could now be very well off. Kass admitted that he hated Richard Christopher for his refusal to pay up. Not that it excuses murder, but I can't say that I blame him for feeling like that."

"So," Laurie surmised, "when Kass eventually had the chance, he sent sick reminders about paying off a debt, and then shot him?"

"He admitted sending the treacle, feathers, and a dead weasel, but not the shooting. Flatly denied it. He keeps ferrets, but says he knew nothing about a recent dead one."

"Then he's a liar," Aunt Madge stated with firm conviction.

My uncle shook his head, contradicted her. "Sadly, no. He had a stout alibi, remember? Joe Kass was here in this hospital the night my brother, Jan's father, was killed. Kass did, however," Uncle continued, "when he was drunk, talk about those gifts he'd sent, and he was *always* on about how much he hated coppers. One in particular."

"The face I saw, and the voice I heard that night in April 1958, wasn't Joe Kass," I stated, sure of myself. Laurie took hold of my trembling hand. "The person I saw decided to repeat what he'd done before. He'd got away with it once, after all."

"I think," Uncle Toby concluded, "that Joe Kass is as shocked as we are that his nephew, then a fifteen-year-old boy with a missing front tooth, which he's since had replaced with a false one, had taken that grief about money, unpaid debt and vitriolic hatred to heart. The boy knew where there was a gun and had known how to use it. He found out where Richard Christopher lived, waited for his Uncle Joe to have a cast iron alibi, and took matters into his own hands. Joe was suspected, but his involvement was completely dismissed. We didn't pursue the matter or search the house – why would we? The pieces of the puzzle, back then, didn't fit together. None of us suspected a boy, Joe's nephew. Maybe if we'd had the slightest inkling, we might have obtained a warrant to search the house, maybe we would have found the gun, but there's nothing to say that Blessit didn't hide it somewhere else until the heat died down. Joe said he kept the thing in an old biscuit tin at the back of his wardrobe, and after doing his bit for King and Country had never looked at it again, even forgotten about it, which I can entirely believe. Many ex-servicemen managed to keep hold of weapons of one sort or another. It probably never occurred to him that his nephew knew the gun existed, let alone where it was kept."

"If I'd remembered everything when I was a child, and told you of them…" I began, but my uncle shook his head.

"We'd have dismissed most of them, Cupcake. You were five. An unreliable witness."

"All the same," I persisted, "had I realised that a missing tooth could be replaced, or thought about the words he spoke to me…"

Laurie raised my hand to his lips, kissed my cold fingers. "It wouldn't have made any difference, sweetheart. It wasn't until Blessit fired that gun this second time that any connection could have been made to the original crime."

Uncle Toby shrugged in a gesture of resignation. "Blessit had taken a dislike to you, Laurie, because you're a policeman, and because Jan prefers you over him. He absorbed Joe's drunken ramblings and those kiddies' nursery rhymes. In particular, Joe's favourite taunt, the one about being poor and the payment of debt, but Joe had only intended to remind my brother about money owed, not to kill him. With Richard dead, that was the end of anything ever being repaid. His murder was as much of a blow to Joe Kass as it was to us."

"I suppose to all intent and purpose," Laurie said, "the items Blessit left, aside from that awful ferret, had no effect on me or Jan. It didn't occur to him that neither of us understood their significance, or the meaning behind *Pop Goes the Weasel*. He assumed, in his unsteady mental state, that we were singing the same tune as he was."

Looking back from where I am now, writing these memoirs of those days in the 1970s, I can't say that I forgave Adrian Blessit for what he did, but my mother and father's life was already upside down, he just hastened their end, that was all. The shame was, Blessit lost his life as well as theirs, for he spent what remained of it in prison. He died of natural causes alone in his cell in 1982. As far as I'm aware, no one attended his funeral.

Personally, I think he didn't understand that nursery rhyme either. To him, a weasel was someone untrustworthy, a thief, and my dad had stolen what should have been his.

If Joe had closed the door on the past and kept it closed, history would have been different and would not have been repeated. Adrian Blessit had most certainly not bargained on a five-year-old girl remembering his face those years later, nor as he'd strolled triumphantly away, leaving his victim, my father, dead in a pool of blood, and my mother with a mind that would never be whole again, that I would, one day, remember what I'd seen, and recall the exact words that he'd uttered at our garden gate.

Good riddance. Pop goes the bloody weasel.

AUTHOR'S NOTE AND ACKNOWLEDGEMENTS

Accuracy. Or rather, lack of it. I'm afraid to say that there was no circus on Chingford Plain in 1973, not until September 1975 was the first Big Top erected there, nor can I remember what the acts were – although there were elephants and camels in 1975, and in later years, definitely lions, for riding along the Plains' bridleways became a test of horsemanship as my daughter, then a young teenager will stoutly confirm. Our pony, Rosie hated the elephants.

My thanks to U.S actor Marty Klebba, a friend of mine, for confirming that it is perfectly acceptable to use the term 'dwarf'. To my shame, I did make that insensitive remark to a small girl during a school visit to the library – I just didn't think!

We did have to contend with library visitors climbing over ladders and pots of paint, despite numerous redirection notices, but thankfully no murders were committed. I have no idea who the decorators were, I do remember having paint dripped on me while I was attempting to shelve books though.

People climbing in through the windows with wheelbarrow-loads of books is indeed an occasional nightmare of mine – even now, after all these years.

Chasneys, a rather nice restaurant opposite Chingford Station did exist (I believe it is a pub now), and I did attend a few functions at the Chingford Assembly Hall, but alas, I can no longer remember what they were – possibly dinner dances, for my dad was a prominent local councillor so, as a family, we went to these functions. I do recall the rather grand foyer (a blue tartan carpet?) and an elaborate, sweeping staircase to the ladies' cloakroom. I can only assume that I didn't particularly enjoy these events to have completely forgotten what they were.

Jonathan Livingston Seagull has remained one of my favourite books – only surpassed by Neil Diamond's film soundtrack and album of the same title. I think because of this story I've always liked seagulls, not despised them as a nuisance.

Coincidentally, while reading through the final version of *A Memory of Murder*, the plea to take care of the rapidly dwindling gull population because of the destruction of their natural habitat and the devastation of Avian Bird Flu, was in the news and mentioned on the BBC *Today* radio programme. Gulls, and many other seabirds, are now close to being put on the endangered species list. We mustn't let gulls become the twenty-first century equivalent of the dodo. Even if seagulls do have a penchant for swooping down to mug people of their chips, sandwiches and other food.

For the record the Wharfdale speakers I mentioned really are mine, and they are still fully functional. (And yes, I did listen to *Dark Side of the Moon* while writing this tale.)

I had better add that our sound-recording librarian during the 1970s was much more amiable than Sy, and he was into Irish folk music, not rock and pop. I had some lovely evenings out with him listening to Irish bands – and I accompanied him to the Royal Albert Hall to see the Chieftains. I wasn't so pleased another time when we missed the last bus one night, and had a long walk home.

I had high heels on.

Pop Goes the Weasel. The explanation for this very old nursery rhyme, which probably started life as a folk song from the 16 or 1700s, is very open to interpretation. I've used the commonest version, and the one most familiar to me.

The unfamiliar Cockney rhyming slang, I confess, I completely 'dog and pup'... made up.

I must mention 'Rave'. The term originated in the 1950s, was used by the Mods in the '60s, fell out of use in the '70s and came back, much changed by electronic music and the 'modern' style of frenetic disco dancing in the 1980s. Bowie mentioned ravers on one of his 1970s tracks.

Thank you to Cathy for the graphics and formatting this book, to Annie for her editing, and Connie, Alison, Anna, Elizabeth St.John and a few of my other reader/writer friends for reading early pre-final edit versions for me. Any missed typos are my fault.

Next time, Jan and Laurie will be visiting Devon for the annual Village Summer Flower and Vegetable Show – *A Mischief of Murder,* which I hope will be written and published soon.

Meanwhile, if you haven't read the first four of the Jan Christopher Cosy Mysteries... why not?

Helen Hollick
Devon 2024

SOUTH CHINGFORD LIBRARY

Photo © Alison Morton

FURTHER PRAISE FOR HELEN HOLLICK'S NOVELS

"Helen Hollick has it all! She tells a great story, gets her history right, and writes consistently readable books" Bernard Cornwell

"A novel of enormous emotional power" Elizabeth Chadwick

"In the sexiest pirate contest, Cpt Jesamiah Acorne gives Jack Sparrow a run for his money!" Sharon K. Penman

"Thanks to Hollick's masterful storytelling Harold's nobility and heroism enthral to the point of engendering hope for a different ending to the famous battle of 1066" Publisher's Weekly

"If only all historical fiction could be this good" Historical Novel Association Reviews

"Most impressive" The Lady

"Helen Hollick's series about piratical hero Jesamiah Acorne and his mystical wife Tiola Oldstagh provides a real comfort read that seamlessly blends history, fantasy, and romance with plenty of action and suspense while also further developing the characters with every new book."

"Loved this book as I have all the previous ones. Good story, excellent characters, well written with just enough descriptive detail of shipboard life and ways."

"I completely gobbled this one up! Captain Jesamiah Acorne has become a bit of an addiction for me."

"I really love this series from Helen Hollick. As usual she is very meticulous with historical facts and as usual you won't be able to put it down."

ABOUT HELEN HOLLICK

First accepted for traditional publication in 1993, Helen became a *USA Today* Bestseller with her historical novel, *The Forever Queen* (titled *A Hollow Crown in the UK)* with the sequel, *Harold the King* (US: *I Am The Chosen King)* being novels that explore the events that led to the Battle of Hastings in 1066.

Her *Pendragon's Banner Trilogy* is a fifth-century version of the Arthurian legend, and she writes a nautical adventure/fantasy series, *The Sea Witch Voyages*. She has also branched out into the quick read novella, 'Cosy Mystery' genre with her *Jan Christopher Murder Mysteries,* set in the 1970s, with the first in the series, *A Mirror Murder* incorporating her, often hilarious, memories of working as a library assistant.

Her non-fiction books are *Pirates: Truth and Tale*s and *Life of A Smuggler*. She is currently writing (spring 2024) about the ghosts of North Devon for Amberley Press.

She lives with her husband and adult daughter in an eighteenth-century farmhouse in North Devon with their dogs and cats, while on the farm there are horses, three fat Exmoor ponies, an old Welsh pony, five geese, several ducks, numerous hens with, occasionally, some sheep and lambs.

And there are a few resident ghosts.

Website: www.helenhollick.net
All Helen's books are available on Amazon:

https://viewauthor.at/HelenHollick
Main Blog:
https://ofhistoryandkings.blogspot.com/
Facebook:
https://www.facebook.com/helen.hollick
X (Twitter): @HelenHollick
https://twitter.com/HelenHollick
public email: author@helenhollick.net

ALSO BY HELEN HOLLICK

THE PENDRAGON'S BANNER TRILOGY

The Kingmaking: Book One

Pendragon's Banner: Book Two

Shadow of the King: Book Three

THE SAXON 1066 SERIES

A Hollow Crown (UK edition title)

The Forever Queen (US edition title. USA Today bestseller)

Harold the King (UK edition title)

I Am The Chosen King (US edition title)

1066 Turned Upside Down

(alternative short stories by various authors)

THE SEA WITCH VOYAGES OF
CAPTAIN JESAMIAH ACORNE

Sea Witch: The first voyage

Pirate Code: The second voyage

Bring It Close: The third voyage

Ripples In The Sand: The fourth voyage

On The Account: The fifth voyage

Gallows Wake: The sixth voyage

To follow

Jamaica Gold, The seventh voyage

*

When The Mermaid Sings

A short read prequel to the Sea Witch Voyages

BETRAYAL

Short stories by various authors

(including a Jesamiah Acorne adventure)

NON-FICTION

Pirates: Truth and Tales

Life Of A Smuggler: In Fact And Fiction

Ghosts of North Devon (expected to be published 2025)

BEFORE YOU GO

How To Say 'Thank you' to your favourite authors (Feedback is so important, and we do appreciate your comments.)

Leave a review on Amazon
https://mybook.to/AMemoryOfMurder
http://viewauthor.at/HelenHollick

'Like' and 'follow' where you can

Subscribe to a newsletter

Buy a copy of your favourite book as a present

Spread the word!